THE PORTOBELLO ROAD

THE

CHEWING GUM

CURTESS
SHOES
LONDON'S KEENEST
SHOESELLERS

PORTOBELLO ROAD

Kay King

ABELARD — SCHUMAN London

6 47 4 8 3

I.S.B.N. 0.200.71743.X

LONDON
Abelard – Schuman
Limited
8 King Street WC2

Made and printed in Great Britain by
Thomas Nelson (Printers) Ltd, London and Edinburgh

CHAPTER ONE

By half-past eight the Portobello Road was becoming busy. As the barrow-boys dragged their stalls into place they glanced up at the clear blue sky and hoped it would stay that way all day. They ripped open crates and boxes and sacks and, kicking the debris into the gutter, began to sort through the fruit, vegetables and flowers. The best they put on one side, and started building pyramids of oranges and apples and pears with the rest. Finally, those they had sorted out were put invitingly into the front ranks while the pyramids concealed the worst. Bananas and bunches of celery were hooked around the tops of the stalls so they looked as if they had suddenly grown green and yellow fingers. More and more mounds of carrots and potatoes were tumbled out onto the wooden boards; cabbages and cauliflowers had their outer leaves torn off, and these were casually tossed in the direction of the already overflowing bins, together with over-ripe tomatoes and mouldy fruit.

The fishmongers began arranging cod and whiting and plaice in decorative patterns and scrolls on their stone slabs. They placed sprigs of parsley here and there and stood back to admire the effect. As the clock on St Peter's Church struck nine the butchers and grocers opened the doors of their shops and the barrow-boys, still chatting to each other, moved towards their stalls and the first of their customers.

This was at the lower end of the road. Higher up and just around the bend the antiques and junk were still being unloaded from cars and vans. Crates and boxes, attaché cases and trunks all disgorged a vast collection of booty. There was silver and china, furniture and pictures, books, jewellery, buttons and old weapons all thrown around in apparent confusion; battered old bowls next to beautifully carved chessmen and Victorian samplers next to Indian shawls. Eventually everything was arranged to the satisfaction of the owners. The stalls were pushed into place and they too settled down to wait for their first customers.

A number of shops had been turned into arcades and these had stalls inside, each crammed with miscellaneous collections of things. Several boys from one of the arcades darted backwards and forwards with cups of tea and coffee from the cafe upstairs.

Gradually the market came to life. Down the lower end people carrying huge shopping baskets began wandering from stall to stall, talking to each other and to the barrow-boys, who were shouting their incomprehensible cries. Money chinked its way from hand to hand, more and more supplies were tipped onto the stalls and gradually it became warmer and warmer. The top end of the road became absolutely packed. People gave up trying to walk along the narrow pavements and began to sprawl across the road. The few cars that ventured down became trapped and the drivers had to inch their way along. There were hundreds of people about: serious shoppers, casual lookers, and people who vaguely hoped they might be tempted into an extravagance.

The whole road began to look as if a huge and dirty tide had swept up it and receded again, leaving a trail of rubbish behind. The pavements were carpeted with paper and the gutters were filled with rotten, squashed fruit and discarded vegetables.

At the stall just around the bend in the road three children stood watching as the owner tipped yet another carton of junk onto it. Everything was left exactly where it fell. Mr Talbot made no effort to sort anything out or to tidy it up. He knew only too well what an attraction a really messy stall had for some people: they were always convinced they were going to come across the bargain of the century.

He frowned as he saw one of the children pick up a plate. "You just leave that alone, Leo," he snapped.

Leo, a small thin boy with ragged brown hair and a pale face, put it down hastily as if it was red hot. He wiped his hands nervously up and down the huge shapeless sweater that nearly reached his knees. "Sorry, Mr Talbot," he said. "I was only looking."

A taller, fair-haired boy moved over. "He wasn't doing anything," he said.

Mr Talbot looked them up and down irritably. "You kids can't keep your hands off anything," he said. "Can't you go and hang round someone else for a change?"

"We just like looking. What's wrong with that?"

Mr Talbot wiped his huge forearm across his face. "Looking's one thing," he said. "Touching's another. He might have dropped it. That's a valuable old plate. Chinese, that is, very old Chinese."

The girl standing by the side of the boys picked it up quickly and flipped it over. "You're right, Mr Talbot," she said, looking up at him from under her lashes. "That's really old. It's the best Woolworth Chinese I've seen. Not many of that period about now." She smiled mockingly at him and strolled off.

7

Mr Talbot's large pink face suddenly turned bright red. "That's enough of your lip, Marie Jenkins," he shouted after her. "You just clear off. You'd better not come back here in a hurry."

Alan and Leo hurried after her. "What do you want to upset him for?" demanded Alan. "You can't blame him for taking care of his stuff."

Leo nodded his head so violently that his hair fell all over his face. " 'Course he's got to keep an eye on it."

"Keep an eye on it!" said Marie incredulously as she pushed her way through the crowds. "You must be joking! If he left it here this Saturday it would all be there next. It's just a load of old rubbish."

"Rubbish or not, it's still his living, isn't it?" said Alan, dodging round a girl with a guitar.

"He's got to live, same as anyone else," said Leo.

"Live!" Marie came to a sudden halt so that Alan cannoned into Leo. "You call that living! All he's got is one rat hole to live in and another to sleep in. You call that living? I'd rather be dead!"

They stared at her. "What a cat!" said Alan to Leo.

"Yeah," said Leo. "What a cat!"

Marie swung round, her long fair hair gleaming in the sunlight. She gave Leo a violent shove so that he slipped into the road. "You make me want to throw up," she spat at him. "You make me want to be sick. Can't you ever think of anything to say for yourself? All you ever do is copy Alan. If he said you were a worm, you'd say you were a worm."

Leo looked embarrassed and stood on one leg and examined the hole in the sole of his plimsoll. There was always a grain of truth in whatever Marie said. "Better than copying you," he mumbled defensively. "All you ever do is go round upsetting people."

"Me!" Marie put her hand to her throat in a dramatic gesture. "Me! I like that! All I ever do is stick up for you in school and now you say . . ."

"I can do without your . . ."

"Why don't you both shut up," said Alan wearily. "I'm not going to waste another Saturday listening to you two bawling each other out." And he started edging his way through the crowds again.

They were separated for a few minutes as a procession of saffron-robed people playing instruments and singing marched up the road. Marie looked at them with interest. "You ought to join them," she said to Leo, looking at their shaven heads, "you'd get a free haircut."

Leo grinned and gave her a friendly jab and then hurried after Alan. Marie, after a moment's hesitation, bustled in front of them both so that it looked as if she was leading.

The three of them now wandered up the road quite happily, occasionally bumping into people, and shouting and waving at people they knew. They stopped at the car parked on the roadside which had books all over the bonnet and on the roof rack. They always did stop there. Alan began reading the titles and fingered the bindings while Leo flicked over pages in a bored sort of way. Marie turned round to the stall behind her and picked up a lace fan. She snapped it open and shut several times, then, since the stall-holder was looking the other way, she began to fan herself vigorously for a minute or two. Then her movements became more languorous. She peered over the top of the fan shyly and hid her face behind it when anyone looked at her. She took to peeping coyly round it, and finally she smiled boldly from beneath it.

Leo looked up from his book and caught sight of her. "What are you making those faces for?" he asked. "You look dafter than ever."

9

Marie snapped the fan shut and tossed it back onto the stall. "I don't know what you're on about," she said casually, but her face was slightly flushed. "I just felt a bit hot," she said.

Leo looked at her sceptically. "You might have felt a bit hot," he said, "but you looked daft."

"Oh, belt up!" snapped Marie. "Come on, Alan, I'm sick of standing here. Let's get on."

Alan put his book down reluctantly. "I wouldn't mind buying that if I had enough money. It was all about old silver and hall-marks and things."

"But you haven't got any old silver," Marie pointed out. "You'd just be chucking your money away."

Alan pushed his hair out of his eyes. "I know I haven't got any old silver, stupid, but I might have some one day and a book like that would come in handy."

Leo nodded in agreement. "You couldn't be done if you had a book like that," he said. "My dad knew a man who'd got an old desk. It wasn't broken or anything like that but it was an old-fashioned thing and he wanted to get rid of it so he'd got room for a new telly. So he went to one of those dealers and asked what he'd give him for it. Well, at last the dealer went round and had a look at it and he said it wasn't worth the trouble of taking it away, but in the end he gave my dad's friend a couple of quid. Then about two weeks later he was going up Kensington Church Street and he was just going past one of those antique shops when he saw it in the window with a sign on it saying a name he'd never heard of. In the end he went in and asked how much it was and . . ."

"How much was it?" asked Marie curiously.

"Guess."

"Twenty pounds," said Marie promptly.

"Thirty-five," said Alan, after a moment's thought.

Leo shook his head. "You're miles out. A hundred and forty guineas!"

"Oh, come off it," cried Marie. "It was only an old desk. You said so yourself. I expect there are new ones that cost that much but not a second-hand one. No one would pay that sort of money for an old one."

Leo licked his finger and drew it across his throat. "See it wet, see it dry," he said.

"It could easily cost that much," said Alan. "Some old stuff's worth a fortune. Just think what they pay for pictures and stamps and things like that. A really good antique could be worth hundreds. It's tough on your dad's friend, though. Did he do anything about it?"

"There wasn't anything he could do, was there?"

"If he was that daft he deserved to be swindled," said Marie. "I mean if you keep your wits about you . . . "

"Like you did over those mystery parcels last Christmas," Leo said. "What was it in yours . . . a plastic whistle and a packet of sweets for five bob . . . and you still wanted to have another go."

Marie went slightly pink. "Oh, that," she said. "I was much younger then."

"It was only last Christmas," Leo reminded her, "and we told you not to waste your money."

Luckily a thin, untidy, black-haired girl appeared on the other side of the road and waved violently at them before they could settle down to another quarrel. "Hey, Marie!" she shouted. "I've been looking for you everywhere."

Marie brightened up immediately. She liked Maggie and, what was more important, Maggie liked her. "Come on," she said to the boys. "I said we'd meet her up in the arcade and have an ice-cream."

Leo hung back. He rubbed one foot against the other.

"Can't," he said awkwardly. "My dad didn't give me any pocket-money."

"I'll pay," shouted Marie, and she wriggled her way into the crowded arcade and thundered up the wooden staircase. "I'll buy yours too, Alan."

By the time Alan and Leo got up there they found Maggie and Marie already sitting at a table with four ice-creams in front of them. "Thanks, Marie," said Leo, attacking his enthusiastically. "It's smashing. Chocolate's my favourite every time."

Alan made a little hole in the centre of his strawberry one and patted the sides with his spoon. "Look," he said. "It's just like a volcano."

"Stop messing around and eat it up," said Marie, and then she turned back to Maggie. "So you've got all the shopping done then?"

Maggie pushed back a long strand of curly hair that was perilously near her mouth. "Well, nearly," she said. "Mum left me ever so much to do but at least I didn't have to cart Bobby around with me. Mrs Taylor's looking after him this morning. I don't half get fed up with him sometimes, though."

"So do we," said Marie gloomily.

"Well, he can't be left alone, can he?" said Alan as he shovelled in another mouthful. "I mean, she couldn't go to work otherwise."

Marie pushed her dish to the centre of the table. "I know, but it's not fair it's always Maggie. Your mum ought to get someone else."

"We wouldn't be any better off if she had to pay someone to look after Bobby," said Maggie. "Mum doesn't go to work because she likes it. She only goes because we need the money."

12

"I know," said Marie. "It just seems hard on you sometimes, Maggie." She rested her chin on her hands. "What shall we do till dinner-time? Got any ideas, Leo?"

Leo looked startled. He wasn't used to being asked what he'd like to do. He looked vaguely up at the ceiling. "I don't know," he mumbled at last. "What do you want to do, Alan?"

Marie groaned. "If I'd wanted to know what Alan wanted to do I'd have asked him myself, stupid."

Alan concentrated on scraping the last of the ice-cream from the bottom of his dish. "I know what I want to do," he said. "I want to go back and have a proper look at that book."

Maggie ran her finger round the inside of her bowl. "That sounds like the most boring idea of the day," she said.

Marie frowned at Maggie. "Don't do that," she said. "It's dirty."

"It's not. And I don't care even if it is. It's my dirt and I like it," Maggie said, and she rubbed her finger even harder round the rim.

"I'm not staying then. It's disgusting," said Marie grandly, and she pushed her chair back and stood up.

"Wait a minute. We're all coming," said Alan hastily, and there was a hideous scraping noise as they all pushed back their chairs and clattered down the staircase. Alan hung back so that he could whisper to Maggie. "What's got into you?" he asked. "What do you want to put her back up for?"

Maggie shrugged. "I don't know. She gets me down sometimes when she comes over all posh. I don't care if she does go off."

However, when they joined the others there was Marie waiting for them smiling happily as if nothing had happened. "I've got a smashing idea," she said. "Let's go up to Bernie's.

We haven't been to see him for ages. He's always got something to look at and as long as we don't make too much row he doesn't mind what we do."

"Yes, let's," cried Alan. "He'd got those smashing old scrapbooks last time."

Maggie began to giggle. "He's sure to have those super clothes still. He'll never know how easily he could sell them if he put them out. He still thinks they're out of date."

"Could he really sell them?" asked Leo. "I mean, they look a bit silly, don't they?"

Marie looked at him scornfully. "Don't you ever notice anything? Half the girls in the Portobello are wearing old clothes now. But if we don't tell Bernie he'll just keep them for us to dress up in." She turned and poked Maggie. "I'm going to put on the beads as well as everything else."

"Oh, all right," said Maggie amiably. "Bags I have the hat with feathers though," and they strolled off arm in arm as if they'd never had a cross word.

"Do you think Bernie's going to let me look at the gramophones again?" asked Leo doubtfully.

"Of course he will," said Alan encouragingly. "Why shouldn't he?"

"Because I broke one of the records last time. He wasn't half mad."

"He'll have got over that. Anyway, we said it wasn't your fault. It was those people who bashed into you."

"But they were customers and we weren't," Leo pointed out, looking downcast. "My dad often bashes me harder for things I haven't done than for things I have done."

"Oh, don't worry," said Alan confidently. "Bernie won't even remember."

He was quite right. Bernie didn't remember. Instead he threw his arms wide and greeted them enthusiastically.

"Lovely," he cried as they crowded into the narrow, dark little shop. "Now all push along into the yard. Mustn't clutter the place up." And they all obediently shunted through the crammed shop and out into the yard which opened into a little alleyway just off the Portobello Road. Here Bernie kept a miscellaneous collection of things like brass bedsteads and cookers and old fridges and worm-eaten furniture.

Bernie himself was a bit like his yard — overflowing. He was a short stocky man, almost bald except for a narrow grey fringe that encircled his perfectly round head. He seemed neckless, so that the back of his head looked as if it hung straight down over his collar. He grabbed Alan and Leo by the arms. "Just the very people I wanted to see," he beamed at them. "I wonder if you could just help me out with a little job." He steered them over to a corner of the yard. "I just want you to lend me a hand with this absolutely superb fireplace. I want to shove it up in the front of the shop so that people can't help seeing it."

It would have been difficult to miss. It was over six feet high and nearly as wide. It was made of dark, highly polished mahogany and right across the top it was carved with strange unrecognizable animals and flowers. Down each side, and curling round the large supporting pillars, were leaves and yet more animals. From the top corners hung angels with folded wings, leering at a huge bird with an open beak that sat on top of the shelf that jutted out a couple of inches.

Maggie and Marie came across to look as the boys helped Bernie to lift it. Marie eyed it with interest. "It's about the ugliest thing I've ever seen," she said conversationally as they staggered out of the yard, down the passage and round to the front of the shop, where they dumped it.

"It is rather nasty," agreed Bernie. He stuck his hands in

his pockets and stood back to gaze at it admiringly. "One might, I think, go so far as to call it hideous."

Alan ran one finger over the bird. "Where did you get it?" he asked.

"From an old mansion in Buckinghamshire," said Bernie promptly.

Maggie looked impressed. "Really!"

"No, not really," confessed Bernie, as he patted it affectionately. "Actually it comes from that dreadful old Victorian house they're pulling down just round the corner. However, one simply must give the customers what they want. And if what they want is a romantic story, then a romantic story is what they shall have." He pulled a crumpled and grimy handkerchief from his pocket and began to flick it up and down the fireplace.

"That's not really very honest, is it?" Maggie said, frowning slightly.

Bernie shook the handkerchief vigorously and stuffed it back into his pocket. "Well," he said, "perhaps not exactly one hundred per cent honest, but then what you've failed to take into account is the happiness that tiny little lie will create. Can't you just see the proud and triumphant owners in their cosy little semi-detached, surrounded by admiring friends and envious neighbours, relating the history . . ."

"It wouldn't look right in a little house," said Leo. "I mean, you wouldn't have much room for anything else, would you?"

"Aha! You've hit the nail on the head, Leo," cried Bernie, ruffling his hair. "You wouldn't *want* anything else." He gazed at the fireplace fondly. "Just one or two of my little footstools perhaps, so that one could rest whilst sitting in awe-struck silence."

Marie was getting tired of all this chatter and was standing just inside the shop picking up and putting down one thing after another. "Can Leo look at the gramophones?" she asked abruptly, and Leo, who would never have dared to ask for himself, shot a look of gratitude at her.

"But of course, my dear, of course." Bernie beamed at her. "Do be careful though, Leo. I really do have a feeling that I might sell one or two today and it really would be too dreadful to miss the chance of lumbering someone else with them. Now tell me, Alan, do you think we've got it in the right spot? I don't want it to be overlooked."

"You can't exactly miss it, can you?" Alan replied as he stepped back.

"Good, good," said Bernie happily as he meandered back into the shop.

They hurried round to the yard at the back again. Leo went straight to the corner where the gramophones were kept and began examining them for the umpteenth time. They fascinated him. There were some with long wriggling horns that looked rather like ugly over-sized flowers, and there were a number with handles sticking out of the sides to wind them up with. There was also a huge pile of old records. But Leo's favourite was a big wooden cabinet that held wax cylinders instead of records. The only time that Bernie had played one for Leo, a thin, wavering voice, sounding as if it was coming from a great distance, had come trickling out of the box. Without Bernie there, Leo didn't actually dare to play anything, so he just shuffled happily through the records.

Maggie and Marie made straight for the battered tin trunk and threw back the lid and dragged out huge quantities of shoes, hats, bags and rags. They sorted through them hastily, their voices getting shriller and shriller with excitement. Bernie had bought the box at an auction together with a lot

17

of other things. When he had opened it and seen just old clothes, he had put it, like so many other things, into the yard and then forgotten about it. It was only when Maggie and Marie were there that they were even taken out.

Within minutes the girls were transformed. "Look at me!" screamed Maggie, twirling round and round in a black-beaded red frock. She suddenly spotted a long piece of fringing and promptly tied it round her waist.

"Don't I look good!" Marie swayed along in front of her on precarious high heels, the buckle of one of them trailing on the ground. She was wearing a completely shapeless violet coloured chiffon frock and was nonchalantly swinging an almost bald feather boa round and round her neck. "Wait a minute." She grabbed hold of a bucket-shaped green hat and jammed it on her head. "Now that's what I call well-dressed. Sorry to put you in the shade again, Maggie, but honestly, you're just plain dowdy."

"No I'm not," said Maggie, diving into the trunk. She hurled a moth-eaten fur bolero round her shoulders and snatched up a beaded bag and a torn parasol and forced her feet into a pair of ancient buttoned boots.

Marie suddenly snatched the parasol from her. "That goes better with my outfit," she said. "I'll have it."

"No you don't! I found it!" exclaimed Maggie, grabbing one end of it. She gave a fierce tug of the handle at the same moment that Marie relinquished it, rocked unsteadily for a moment or two and fell on top of Alan, who was standing just behind her. He dropped his book.

"Why don't you shut up!" he said crossly. "All you girls ever do is scream and fight. Bernie'll turn us all out if you keep on making a row like that."

Marie stuck her tongue out at him. "You aren't half a misery," she said. "And anyway," she twisted the ends of her hair round one finger, "you haven't got anything to worry about. You know Bernie likes me." She suddenly smiled charmingly and waved her hand at Bernie who was scurrying past the entrance to the yard. He stopped and then came in.

"My dear Marie," he cried. "Now you really do make a lovely picture standing there. What a pity you can't spend the rest of the day with me. People would flock in, you know, simply flock in."

"You could prop her up next to the fireplace," Maggie muttered.

Bernie spun Marie round. "You know, you look absolutely ravishing dressed like that. We'd sell everything in a flash if you simply modelled these clothes for me. It might even become the thing, you know, to dress at Bernie's. People might think it rather chic." He turned to Alan. "What do you think? Could it catch on?"

Marie and Maggie looked at each other significantly and began to strip off the clothes as fast as they could. The last thing they wanted was to see them sold. As Maggie slammed the lid of the tin box, Marie popped up in front of Bernie again. "Oh, Bernie," she said, untruthfully. "I wish I could just stay here with you, but I've got to go. It's my mum, you know."

Bernie stroked her fair hair. He had some vague idea that Marie's mother was a frail, helpless woman who constantly needed Marie's help and support. He sighed. "I suppose I must let you go then. I can hardly be selfish and keep you under the circumstances. But you must promise to come back with your friends. It brightens things up so when you're around."

He smiled at them all as they went out of the yard shouting thank-yous and goodbyes to him and then he padded round to the front again to admire the fireplace.

"It must be nearly dinner-time," Marie remarked. "I'm starving."

Maggie looked horrified. "It can't be! Mum'll go mad. I'm supposed to have done the potatoes and bought the meat pies and picked up Bobby. Gosh!" She pelted down the road, her long hair streaming out behind her.

"Hey! Maggie! What about this afternoon? Are we going to the pictures like we said?" Marie shouted after her. But Maggie didn't even bother to look back.

"Poor old Maggie," said Alan. "She has it tough, doesn't she? She's always helping in the house or doing the shopping or looking after Bobby. Still, I suppose it can't be helped."

"She might have said what she's doing this afternoon," grumbled Marie. "I suppose I'm supposed to hang around all day waiting for her."

"Talk about selfish!" Alan looked upwards despairingly. "Why don't you try just for once thinking about someone else besides the precious Miss Jenkins."

"And why don't you just mind your own business!" retorted Marie.

Alan went bright pink. "Why don't you . . ."

"Forgot all about me, didn't you?" said a reproachful voice and they both turned round to look at Leo.

Alan clapped him on the back. "We didn't exactly forget about you . . ."

"We just happened to leave you behind," finished Marie.

Alan glared at her. "If you don't shut up, Marie," he said threateningly, "your mother's going to hear in an accidental sort of way that you stick on mascara and all that stuff when she's not around."

"I'm only practising. You know I'm only practising. And I don't go out in it anyway. And anyway, what I said to Leo was only a joke. You knew it was only a joke, didn't you, Leo?"

Leo looked uncomfortable. He didn't want Alan and Marie quarrelling over him but he also knew that Marie had meant what she said. But then, you never knew where you were with Marie. One minute she was all over you and the next minute she was giving you the cold shoulder. At last, however, he managed a weak grin. "It's O.K., Alan," he said. "She doesn't mean half of what she says."

"There you are then," said Marie triumphantly. "If he doesn't care then why should you."

Alan shrugged. "See you after dinner then. Coming, Leo?"

"He's coming with me," said Marie firmly. "I'm going to take him home for dinner. His dad won't have got him anything, will he, Leo?"

Leo shook his head. Since his mother had died he hardly ever had proper meals. Sometimes his dad would send him out for fish and chips or they would open a tin, but often they just had bread and cheese. "Won't your mum mind?" he asked nervously.

"Of course she will," said Marie, "but she'll still give you something to eat. Right then, Alan. See you outside the pictures then."

Alan looked up at the cloudless sky. "Can't say I'm keen on the pictures," he said. "It seems a waste on a day like this."

"It'll be pouring this afternoon," said Marie with absolute certainty. "It's Saturday, isn't it? Anyway, let's meet at about half past two. We can make our minds up then. Besides, Maggie's sure to go there to look for us and she won't half be fed up if we're not there."

"All right then," agreed Alan. "See you outside the pictures."

"So long!" shouted Marie as she went off in the other direction dragging Leo behind her.

CHAPTER TWO

Marie strode along the road while Leo shuffled rather nervously behind her. He'd never met Marie's mother but he'd heard enough about her. She'd got a mania for having everything neat and shining and clean around her and he was realistic enough to know that he didn't fit into any of those categories.

Suddenly Marie noticed how far behind he was. She halted for a moment to let him catch her up. "Come on, Leo!" she exclaimed impatiently. "Can't you get a move on? We're late enough already."

"What'll she say when she sees me?"

Marie shrugged. "How should I know? Who cares, anyway? As long as you're not rude or anything she'll put up with you. Greg and me get away with murder sometimes as long as we keep sounding polite, specially in front of the neighbours. Greg broke the kitchen window the other day but because he told her in front of some visitors and kept saying how sorry he was she didn't really say anything except 'Don't do it again, Greg'. Gosh, you won't get me being taken in by my kids, I can tell you."

Leo remained silent. He knew what would happen to him if he ever broke a window. His father would thump him straight away whether anyone was there or not. Some people, thought Leo, sighing to himself, just don't know when they're well off.

They had by this time got almost to the bottom of the Portobello Road and they turned into a side street. Leo hadn't actually been to the house before but he automatically came to a halt in front of the neatest house in the road. Everything about it shone. The door handle shone. The knocker shone. The bell shone. The paint gleamed. The windows glittered. Even the flowers in the narrow front garden stood in orderly ranks, each separate plant coming into flower at exactly the same time. White net curtains, elaborately draped across the windows, successfully prevented anyone from seeing in and no doubt equally successfully prevented anyone from seeing out.

Marie seized the gleaming knocker and banged loudly on the door, at the same time shouting impatiently through the letter-box. There was a quick pattering as someone came up the passage and Leo hastily tried to comb his tangled hair with his fingers whilst rubbing the soles of his plimsolls up and down the legs of his dirty jeans.

The door opened a crack and Mrs Jenkins peeped through it before opening it wide enough for them to come in. She was a thin, neat woman with her hair tied up in a scarf and she was wearing a brightly-coloured overall. "You're late, Marie," she said accusingly. "Your dinner's been ready for ages." Suddenly she saw Leo, who was half-hidden behind Marie. "And who's that might I ask?" She pushed Marie on one side and shot a quick look up and down Leo. "He's not a friend of yours, surely. I've told you more than once, Marie, that I won't have you bringing any Tom, Dick or Harry into this house. You can't be too careful these days."

"Oh, Mum, you are awful," said Marie, holding Leo firmly

by the sweater in case he thought of running away. "I've told you about him lots of times. It's Leo."

Mrs Jenkins looked him over doubtfully and Leo, now fully aware that he really did look scruffy, tried to hide the hole in the sleeve of his sweater, and appeared to concentrate on standing on one leg. "It's all right, Marie," he muttered. "I ought to be getting back. Dad might wonder where I am."

Marie tugged him inside. "Your dad wouldn't notice if you didn't go back till next year." She turned to her mother again. "I've told you about him," she repeated. "He's the one who hasn't got a mother and he's just as hungry as I am."

Mrs Jenkins shot one more sharp look at him. "All right, bring him in," she said grudgingly. "If he hasn't got a mother it's not his fault, I suppose." She led the way down the narrow passage to the back of the house while Marie grinned encouragingly at Leo and gave him a friendly pinch. Mrs Jenkins stopped at the kitchen door and swung round again to address herself directly to Leo. "You'll not sit down in my kitchen, young man, not till you've got rid of all that filth on your face and hands. Take him into the scullery, Marie, and see that he washes himself properly. And you can take off that pullover right now." She held out her hand for it while Leo, by now bright red, struggled out of it. She regarded it with disgust. "Look at all those holes. Really disgraceful, that's what it is. You ought to be ashamed, wearing something like that, you really ought."

Marie pushed Leo ahead of her into the scullery. She turned the taps on. "Don't take any notice of her," she whispered as she handed Leo a towel. "She always goes on like that. She can't help it."

"Stop whispering, Marie," her mother called out. "It's rude to whisper. If I've told you once, I've told you a hundred times not to do it."

24

Leo stood at the scullery sink and scrubbed both his hands and face so hard that Marie began to wonder whether his skin could take much more punishment. He dried himself and then tugged painfully at his hair with a comb that Marie thrust into his hands. Finally he soaked it with water and then parted it carefully and sleeked it down. "How do I look?" he asked anxiously.

"Like something the cat's brought in," she said cheerfully.

"That's not a nice thing to say to anyone, Marie," said her mother reprovingly as she came to look Leo over. "I really don't know where you pick up those common expressions. Your father's going to be very disappointed in you when he gets back on leave. Sometimes you sound as if you've been brought up in the gutter."

Marie waited patiently until her mother had finished. "We're ever so hungry," she said.

Mrs Jenkins gave Leo a quick look. "I must say you look a different boy," she said approvingly. "Soap and water never did hurt anyone, you know. Go on into the kitchen then. Your dinner's on the table. Go and have it while it's hot." She fumbled in a drawer and brought out some darning wool and a needle and settled down in an armchair while Leo and Marie sat down at the kitchen table.

"Mum," said Marie, prodding a potato with her fork, "can I go to the pictures this afternoon?"

"On a day like this? It's lovely out. Why don't you go into the park instead? It would do you a lot more good."

"I'm fed up with the park. You can't do anything there."

"What do you want to do?"

"Oh, you know what I mean," explained Marie. "It's just that it's full of notices saying you can't. I reckon they've got a special man there to see what people are doing and then he whips off and makes a notice saying they can't."

"You do talk a lot of nonsense." Mrs Jenkins looked critically at her darning. "Nobody puts up notices without a good reason and if people make rules then you children ought to stick to them. Anyway, it's much better for you to be out in the fresh air, even if you just go for a nice walk, than to be cooped up in a nasty stuffy cinema. I must say I don't care for the look of the children I see coming out at all. They're not the sort I want you mixing with. You'd be much better off playing a nice quiet game in the park with some friends."

She looked up sharply. "Leo! Don't stuff so much in your mouth at once. It's not polite. And there's no need to hold on to your knife and fork all the time. No one's going to take them away from you." She glanced at Marie. "You can take that sulky look off your face, young lady. I'm not giving you the money for the pictures so you might as well make up your mind to it. It's about time you learned you can't always have everything you want."

"Oh, Mum," said Marie in a wheedling voice, "go on.· Don't be mean. I'll do the washing-up for you tonight if you'll let me go."

"You'll do the washing-up anyway. I'm not running a hotel, my girl."

Marie leapt up from the table and flung her arms around her mother while Leo gazed in amazement. He knew just what he'd get from his father if he carried on like that. "Please Mum," she said coaxingly, "it's a smashing old film. It's called 'How to Marry a Millionaire'."

"Mind that needle, Marie," said her mother. "The way you carry on you'll need to marry one. I'm not made of money you know. You're always wanting money for this and money for that. It's about time you realised money doesn't grow on trees."

Marie perched on the edge of her mother's chair, her arm around her neck. "Couldn't you look on it as an investment?" she said. "You know if I did marry one the first thing I'd do would be to buy you a really super fur coat. I can just see you in a long white dress with the coat just slung round your shoulders as if it didn't matter if it fell off, nodding at your chauffeur as you get in the car."

Mrs Jenkins touched the top of her turban with her fingers and then ran them down her overall. "I dare say I could look as well as the next," she said complacently, "if only I had the time and the money. Mark you, I'd look after my things a bit better than some of them do, I can tell you that. You can't open a paper these days without reading about robberies. There was one only this morning. A jeweller who has a little shop in one of those hotels had some bracelets and a necklace stolen only yesterday. Mind you, it served him right, it really did."

"What were they worth?" asked Marie.

"Forty thousand, that's what it said. They were rubies. They must have been lovely, but how he could have been so stupid as to leave them with customers, I really don't know. I wouldn't even leave my wedding ring with strangers let alone . . ."

"What happened?" interrupted Marie.

"Well, you know that new hotel near the park?" Marie nodded. "They had a guest who was staying there — you know the sort, well-spoken and well-dressed — well, he stayed there for some time with his wife and spent quite a lot of money. He had the best suite and he always paid his bills immediately and he was generous with tips to the staff. He liked the man in the jeweller's and he bought several things from him, not large things but not cheap. Well, finally he mentioned he wanted to buy a necklace or something like

27

that for his wife's birthday and so the jeweller got several things for him to look at, but he couldn't really make up his mind. He said his wife, who was ill in bed, would have to choose for herself, but that he was pretty sure she would choose the rubies. Then the manager said would he like to show them to her. He hummed and hawed for a few minutes, and then let himself be persuaded by the manager. Off he went in the lift and that was the last they saw of him, or his wife, or the jewels. They just cleared out leaving all their things behind them."

"That was a smart bit of work!" cried Marie in admiration. "What a nerve!"

"Really, Marie! What a way to speak. They were thieves, just thieves. There's nothing smart about that."

"No, I didn't mean that," said Marie hastily. "I only meant they must have been smart people to stay in a place like that and get away with it. No," she went on righteously, "it's awful to steal like that. Still, I expect they'll be caught."

Leo, who was still eating, looked up and nodded. "I bet it's hard to get rid of stuff like that. They won't be able to sell it straight away. They'll have to keep it hidden until things have cooled a bit."

Mrs Jenkins broke off another piece of wool and attacked the next hole. "I hope they are caught," she said fiercely. "I don't hold with all this stealing and shooting and stabbing. It's time they stopped it. Perhaps someone will give them away." She examined the sweater carefully. "Now that looks a bit better, Leo. Really," she went on, "you hardly feel safe in your own home these days and the telly doesn't help, what with fighting and violence every five minutes and boxing and wrestling and calling it sport. When I was a girl sport meant running races once a year with girls wearing proper divided skirts instead of those tight little knickers they all have these days. It makes you wonder what the world's coming to."

Marie had been getting more and more bored during this familiar tirade so she bent over her mother and gave her a quick kiss. "Mum," she said, "we're ever so late. Can I have the money and go?"

Grumbling as she did so, Mrs Jenkins fumbled in her bag while Leo scoffed down the last piece of apple tart. Suddenly Mrs Jenkins thrust the sweater at him. "I've done the best I can with it," she said, "but it's beginning to look as if it's only made of darns. It's about time you had a new one and you can tell your father I said so."

Leo began stammering thanks to Mrs Jenkins, but before he could finish — and indeed he'd become so tangled up he didn't quite know how he was ever going to — Marie grabbed his arm and towed him out of the house. "Hurry up!" she said urgently, slamming the front door behind her. "The others will go in without us if we don't get a move on."

"I can't go anyway," panted Leo, as he rushed behind her. "I told you. My dad forgot to give me any pocket money."

"It'd be a miracle if he remembered," said Marie tartly. "Still, I got enough for both of us from mum. I told her I didn't want to sit with scruffy kids in the front so she gave me some extra. Didn't you see?"

They were both out of breath by now so they dropped into a trot as they entered the crowded market. "I don't think I ought to take her money really," said Leo, sounding slightly bothered. "She was ever so nice to me. Look at my sweater."

"No thank you," said Marie. "Anyway, don't be so daft. It's not her money now, it's mine."

"But you only got it by lying."

"So what," said Marie carelessly. "Look, it was me who told the lie, not you, and anyway it made her happy. What

29

does it matter whether I spend the money on one seat or two? She won't know and what she doesn't know won't hurt her. It just makes her feel good to think we can have better things than anybody else because then she can pretend we are better than anybody else. I only did it for you, Leo. I thought you wanted to come to the pictures with me. Still, if you don't . . ." She turned slightly away from him, and Leo thought he could tell from the drag of her shoulders that he had hurt her.

"Sorry, Marie," he said awkwardly. "Somehow it didn't seem right not . . ."

Marie shrugged. "Please yourself," she said. "It doesn't make any difference to me." Suddenly she spotted Maggie and waved. "Look — she's waiting. Alan's behind her and — oh, crikey!" She groaned loudly. "That's torn it. She's got Bobby with her. That's just about the end. We'll never get into the pictures with him there. Honestly, all she does is drag him around with her these days. "Maggie! Maggie!" she shouted. "Can't you take Bobby home? He'll be in the way."

"No I can't," Maggie screamed back. "There's no one else to look after him so Mum said I'd got to." She gave him a good shake as Maggie and Leo joined her. "He'll be good, won't you, Bobby?"

Bobby stood there stolidly sucking an ice-lolly, completely unaffected by the shaking and the shouting. He was only just five years old and he was quite used to being unwanted by Maggie's friends and equally unmoved by it. He knew that Maggie would never leave him and he also knew that the others, no matter how much they complained, would always put up with him.

Marie scowled down at him. "You know we can't get into the pictures with him here." She leaned against a poster and moodily began to tear a strip from it. "You are the limit, Maggie. What have we got to cart him around for?"

"I told you," said Maggie. "There isn't anyone else. It's not my fault. You don't think I wanted to bring him, do you?"

Alan tugged fairly gently at Bobby's hair. "He's not doing any harm," he said. "What difference does it make if he's here. We wouldn't have minded if you'd brought Greg with you, Marie."

"You wouldn't, but he would," said Marie nastily. "Now we're properly stuck. You know what old Walker's like now he's the manager. He's not going to let us slip Bobby in. I bet he hasn't forgotten what happened last time. We all got chucked out when Bobby started screaming."

"Whose fault was that?" said Alan. "I told you Bobby wouldn't like a horror film and you wouldn't listen."

"I told you too," said Leo.

Marie shot withering looks at both of them. "He'd have been all right if you two hadn't gone on and on about it being a horror film. He wouldn't have noticed. Now what are we going to do?" She gloomily tore off another strip of the poster.

"Walker's tough," said Maggie. "He won't let anyone get away with anything."

"That's why they made him the manager," said Alan. "Remember what it used to be like?"

"Yes," said Marie. "Smashing."

"Well," said Alan, taking no notice of her, "since we can't get in we'll have to think of something else."

They stood there for a long time arguing with each other. No two of them wanted to do the same thing and yet they didn't really want to do anything on their own. Their voices became louder and louder and they were becoming more and more quarrelsome when Fred, the tallest, the heaviest, the slowest and the most good-natured boy in the school joined them.

He beamed at them all. "Are you going in too?" he asked, delighted to have company. "I was thinking of it but I don't like going on my own. I like someone to talk to."

"Bad luck then," said Marie. She pointed to Bobby who had finished the ice-lolly but was still hopefully sucking the stick. "We're stuck. We can't go because of him."

"I don't suppose the film was much good," said Fred. "Let's go round the market instead."

Marie raised her eyebrows. "Brilliant," she said sarcastically, "really brilliant. I don't know how you manage to keep coming out with such good ideas."

Fred smiled modestly. "I don't know either," he said. "They just sort of come into my head."

"You've got a head like a . . ." snorted Marie, but she was interrupted by the sudden shrilling of bells and they all rushed to the edge of the pavement. A police car swept down the road, the driver skilfully weaving his way between cars, pedestrians, carts and ponies. At the same time two policemen roared round the corner on motorbikes while three constables appeared as if from nowhere. They all converged on one of the stalls. The children rushed excitedly across the road towards it, only to be kept back by the stiff arm of a policeman. They could see practically nothing as the crowd got larger and larger and could only hear the occasional official words "Charge you . . . at the station . . . wouldn't say anything now if I were you" before they were moved quite a long way back by the police. Bobby gave a quick look round, wriggled under a policeman's arm and disappeared from view.

"What's happened?" Marie shouted at the nearest policeman. "Are you putting him inside?"

"Who is it?"

"What's he done?"

The crowd, now a considerable size, began to hum with excitement, speculating and passing on rumours to each other. The police, very experienced at their job, soon persuaded the crowd not only to move back but to begin to disperse. The children, however, managed to stay nearby. They saw the whole of the dealer's stock being put inside the boot of the police car and the man himself being helped inside.

"I don't know how it got there," he protested. "Anyone could have dropped it on my stall without me noticing. I've got a good name round here. Ask anybody."

"I should save it all for the station," said a constable, getting in beside him, and the police car sped off. The speed cops adjusted their goggles and roared away and the remainder of the crowd hung round for a bit. The children watched with great pleasure as two of the constables, looking rather self-conscious, wheeled the barrow away, followed by cries of "Trying to turn an honest copper, then?"

Suddenly Maggie grabbed Maggie's arm. "Where's Bobby?" she asked. She looked round anxiously. "I can't see him anywhere, can you, Marie?"

They began peering through the crowds. Alan immediately rushed up to the next corner and stared up and down. "He's not up here," he shouted. "Leo, you and Fred go up to the top of the Portobello and look for him and I'll go down. You and Marie stay there, Maggie, in case he comes back on his own."

Leo and Fred trotted off together. "I'll go back to the

pictures," said Fred. "He might have thought we were going in after all."

Maggie clung on to Marie's arm looking as if she was going to burst into tears. She pulled out a crumpled handkerchief and blew her nose loudly. "I don't know what mum'll say," she sniffed. "I can't go back without him. I didn't see him slip away. Anything might have happened to him," and she twisted and untwisted the handkerchief anxiously.

"Don't be silly," said Marie. "Fancy getting worked up like that! Anyone would think he'd been missing all day instead of five minutes. Anyway, he knows his way round here like the back of his hand."

Maggie brushed at the tears that were forming in the corners of her eyes. "It's all right for you," she said. "He's not your little brother."

"Thank heaven!" said Marie.

"You haven't got to face my mum and say you lost him."

"Oh, come off it, Maggie," said Marie impatiently. "He won't come to any harm. Haven't you heard the devil takes care of his own?"

"How can you . . ." began Maggie, and then she broke off and darted through the crowd. "There he is!" she shouted and rushed into a shop doorway. He was standing by a man whose back was towards them. Maggie swooped down and grabbed him. "You naughty little boy," she cried. "Fancy wandering off like that on your own!" and she alternately shook and hugged him. "Mum would skin you alive if she knew, so you'd better not tell her." She gave him another little shake. "Do you understand, Bobby? She'd better not know."

Marie had by now managed to make the boys understand that they'd found Bobby. They came panting back and looked very relieved to see him clutching Maggie's hand again.

"You mustn't go off like that, Bobby," said Leo earnestly. "It's naughty."

Bobby stared at him impassively.

"What's he holding?" asked Alan, and they all turned and stared at the bundle of rags he had half-hidden under his jumper. Bobby clutched anxiously at it with his free hand.

"Throw it away, whatever it is," said Maggie. "I bet it's full of nasty germs, Bobby, and they'll make you ill." Bobby took no notice. "Come on," she said, holding out her hand. "Give it to me."

Bobby shook his head and snatched his other hand away from Maggie's so that he was now able to clutch his bundle with two hands. "Let me have a look," she said impatiently, and then, giving a sudden jerk, she got possession of it.

"What is it?" asked Marie curiously as they all crowded round.

Maggie shook it out. She was holding the hem of a tattered and rather tawdry velvet dress. From the neck of the dress hung a wooden head. Marie flipped it so that it was upright and they could have a proper look. It was a grotesque doll's face. It had an enormously long beaky nose with the tip missing, a long pointed chin, a grinning mouth and reddish-coloured hair made out of string. Two stuffed arms hung down helplessly at the side.

"It's a sort of puppet," said Alan suddenly. "Don't you remember making them with Miss Williams?"

"That's it," cried Leo. "It's a puppet."

"It's about the dirtiest puppet in the world," said Marie, holding her nose. "It stinks. You'd better chuck it in the nearest dustbin, Maggie. I shouldn't like to think where it's been."

"It doesn't actually stink," said Maggie. "It's just plain filthy."

"It's a bit like Miss Williams, isn't it?" said Fred. "I mean when you look at it properly you can see. She's got a nose like that too."

Alan stared at it critically. "She wasn't actually quite as bad as that," he said. "Anyway, she couldn't help her nose."

"Why don't you make him throw it away, Maggie?" asked Marie. "I don't suppose Bobby really wants it and you don't want to carry it home, do you?"

Maggie hesitated for a moment and glanced down at Bobby. He stared up at her. "You lost me," he said simply. "I'll tell mum you lost me."

Maggie looked flabbergasted. "*I* lost you! I like that! You cunning little devil. You know it was you who lost me. It was all your own fault." Bobby continued to stare at her. "Anyway, I wasn't going to throw it away," she said. "You'll jolly well have to carry it home yourself. I'm not going to. Here, take it!" and she thrust the puppet back into his arms. "Marvellous, isn't it!" she went on, turning to the others, "the way he's reached five already. You'd have thought someone would have throttled him by now."

"I don't know," said Fred. "I don't see why he shouldn't keep it. In a way, he's right. I mean, you lost him as much as he lost you, really."

"It's only a bit dirty," said Alan. "It looks old though. They don't make puppets like that now."

"Thank goodness!" said Marie.

Maggie looked up and frowned. "Let's go," she said. "There's that Ann Lucas coming along and I don't want to talk to her. Ever since they picked her to be the princess in the school play she acts as though you ought to curtsey to her whenever she passes."

"Is she really going to be the princess?" asked Alan. "She must be good or Miss Fisher wouldn't have chosen her."

"What play?" asked Fred. "I didn't know there was going to be a play."

Marie raised her eyes to the sky and spread her arms in a wide dramatic movement. "And where were you Fred Rogers when they gave out ears and eyes? It's been going on for about a month now. They started rehearsing ages ago. Hadn't you noticed anything going on?"

As they all straggled off in the direction of Maggie's home Fred suddenly asked Marie, "Why didn't they choose you then?"

"What for?" asked Leo.

"For the princess," said Fred. "I mean, Marie's got yellow hair and everything."

"Marie was away when they cast the play," said Maggie. "You'd got a cold or something, hadn't you, Marie?"

"Not really," said Marie, "but you know what my mum's like. I've only got to blow my nose and she thinks I've got pneumonia."

"I bet you'd have been chosen otherwise," said Maggie. "You'd have been better than Ann Lucas any day."

They came to a halt by Maggie's front door. She looked at them all and then quite suddenly pushed Bobby up the steps. "Sorry," she said. "It's been a rotten afternoon. It's all his fault. He's just been a pain in the neck. Say you're sorry, Bobby."

Bobby stood on the top of the steps and stared down at them all thoughtfully for a moment. He shook his head and waggled the puppet at them instead. Maggie raised her eyebrows and shrugged. "Sorry," she said again.

"See you on Monday then," said Marie. "Can't see you tomorrow because I've got to go and see my grandmother in Kilburn, worse luck." She wandered off down the road with the boys. "I hate going there. She never likes what I wear or

37

what I say or what I do or what I eat or where I go. I don't know why she ever wants to see me."

"You're lucky to have a grandmother," said Leo. "All I've got is my dad and he's hardly ever there."

Marie peeled off from the boys as they reached her turning and she waved goodbye to them. "Tootle-oo," she said. "See you on Monday."

The boys went back to the Portobello Road, now almost empty. The excitement had died down and there were very few people about. Leo went and stood where the police car had stopped. "I wonder what he was up to," he said.

Alan shrugged. "Could have been anything."

"It was about a jewel case," said Fred. "It hadn't got anything in it though."

"It couldn't have been about an empty jewel case," said Leo scornfully. "It was probably about something else — like drugs or spies . . ."

"Selling stolen goods probably," said Alan.

"Anyway it was a bit of excitement," said Fred.

"The only bit of excitement that ever seems to happen to me is going to school," Alan remarked. "Still, at least Monday can't possibly be as dull as today."

"Not if the head's in a swishing mood," said Fred gloomily, "and he usually is on Mondays."

CHAPTER THREE

They all met in the playground before morning school on Monday, but they hardly had time to speak to each other before the head-boy appeared clanging his bell loudly and they had to go to their classrooms. Maggie and Marie were in fact in the same class but their form teacher saw to it that they were kept apart as much as possible, otherwise they would have got no work done at all. In fact they could only see each other when Marie turned round completely in her seat. However, as they were lining up to go into prayers Marie did manage to hiss to Maggie, "Did Bobby tell your mother you'd lost him?"

"No," whispered Maggie, "but I didn't half have a job getting her to let him keep the puppet. I'll tell you about it later when . . ."

"Margaret Hobbs!" Mr Marsh stood over her and looked cross. He waggled his finger in her face. "It's Monday. It's still only Monday. Let's try to last out until Tuesday this week before we get really annoyed with each other." He turned away just in time to catch Marie making a sympathetic face at Maggie. He shook his finger at her. "That goes for you too, Marie," he said. "You can aim for Tuesday as well."

Just then the tail end of the class next to them filed past and much to the girls' relief Mr Marsh gave the signal for theirs to follow on behind. In the hall Leo and Fred beamed at Maggie and Marie but Alan, a form prefect and therefore very conscious of his dignity, pretended not to see them. Assembly took its normal course, and then the head gave his usual Monday morning pep talk. Marie gazed at him with wide-open blue eyes and didn't hear a word he said. She vaguely knew he was droning on about water-pistols and the state of the playground and about smoking, but her mind was full of other, and to her, far more important things.

During the normal uproar that preceded any lesson Marie did manage to shout to Maggie above the din of slammed desk lids and the scraping of chairs, "Did you read about that chap who got pinched? It was all in the papers . . . " but then, as Mr Marsh entered for their English lesson, she broke off abruptly and hastily got out her text books.

It wasn't until dinner-time that they got together again, and as they sat waiting for their turn to go to the serving hatch, Marie told them all about the report she'd seen in the newspaper. "This chap," she said excitedly, "had got this little leather case hidden under a lot of junk on his stall and somebody must have tipped the cops off because they knew exactly where to look."

Fred nodded. "That's what I told Alan and Leo. I said they'd found a jewel case. I knew before you." He looked very pleased with himself.

Marie began to feel annoyed and she half-turned her back on him. "Well, the jeweller has identified the case as being the one he left with the bloke in the hotel . . . "

"What hotel?" asked Fred.

"The one they were staying at of course, stupid."

"Who was?"

"He was and the woman, only she hardly came into it. Anyway, it was the right case but they didn't find the necklace or the bracelets so I suppose they've got away with them."

"What necklace?"

Marie glanced at Fred and tapped her head significantly. "He's just not right up there, you know," she said to Maggie. "He must have a bit missing."

"Oh, shut up," said Alan and he began to explain about the theft to Fred.

Marie went on gabbling to Maggie. "Anyway, the dealer's been kept at the police station — helping enquiries, they say, and I suppose they'll charge him. I expect he'll spill the beans in the end."

"He might have been telling the truth, I suppose," said Maggie. "I mean, someone could have hidden the case on his barrow when he wasn't looking, so it doesn't really prove he was in the gang, does it?"

Marie looked scornful. "I bet he has his eyes glued to his stall all day long just in case anyone tries to pinch anything. They all do. I bet he didn't move an inch from it."

"I guess he'll come clean when the cops put the heat on," drawled Leo, in what he fondly imagined was an American accent, "and then . . ." but the rest of what he was saying was lost as, with a tremendous scraping of chairs, their table rose to join the queue at the serving hatch. By the time they returned with piled plates Maggie and Marie were already talking about something else.

"That rotten old Bobby told my mum he'd had a super time with us and my mum said I'd got to take him again," Maggie was complaining. "I told her it wasn't fair on all of you but she said it couldn't be helped. Honestly, I'm sick of dragging him around with me."

41

"Don't be daft, Maggie," said Alan. "It can't be helped. We hardly go anywhere that matters anyway. We don't mind, do we?" he said, looking at the rest.

Leo stared down at his plate and shrugged. Fred, his mouth full, shook his head slowly from side to side while Marie slammed down her knife and fork. "Well I mind," she said. "If Maggie's got to take him then she's got to take him and we've got to put up with it. But I'm not going to pretend that I don't mind because I do. And I'm telling you now that if he keeps on running away then I'm not looking for him. He can stay lost for all I care," and she picked up her fork and dug it viciously into a potato.

"The way you go on you'd think he was always running away," said Maggie indignantly. She pushed her hair out of her way. "It's the first time he's ever done it. He doesn't even like strangers. When I was taking him to school this morning some man said hello and Bobby wouldn't even answer. He just hung on to that stupid old puppet with one hand and grabbed me with the other. I keep telling him it's rude not to answer when he's spoken to but he just gets stubborn and sucks in his lips."

"I don't think you ought to encourage him to talk to strangers," said Alan. "After all, you don't know who they are or what they want."

"What on earth would they want with Bobby?" demanded Marie.

Leo ran his fork round his empty plate just to make sure he hadn't missed anything. "You're not always right, Marie," he said.

"I nearly always am," she said complacently as she stacked the dirty plates and took them away. She came back and looked in a disgusted way at her pudding. "Jam tart again. I bet cook really flogged her brain to think this one up. I bet it's as hard as nails too. Just look. Bright red tart in a bright yellow sea. It practically turns me up to look at it. I hate custard."

"I love it," said Leo eagerly.

"Pass your plate over," Marie said promptly and she transferred as much as she could from her plate to his. "There you are then. Don't blame me if you wake up and find yourself all slit-eyed in the morning. Still, maybe yellow suits you."

Leo decided to treat this as an insult and flicked a piece of jam tart at her. He missed but the teacher on duty spotted him. "Leo Chandler!" he roared. "Come here!" Leo got to his feet and stood dejectedly in front of the teacher while the whole room fell silent. "You really are a disgusting boy! I have no doubt that flicking food is simply part of your normal behaviour at home but this is something that I will not tolerate here. Do you do it at home?" Leo stared at his feet. He raised Leo's chin. "Well, do you?"

"No, Mr Peters," mumbled Leo.

"Then why do it here?"

Marie jumped to her feet. "It was my fault, Mr Peters," she said. "I was pulling his leg . . ."

"A really remarkable feat, my dear Marie, since you are at one end of the table and Leo is at the other." A few people sniggered at this and Marie's eyes flashed round noting where they came from. She made a mental note to get her own back at some time.

"She didn't really *pull* my leg," Leo said earnestly. "It was . . ."

"Leo," said Mr Peters in a weary voice, "sometimes you are just a very silly little boy. Just go away from me — but remember, if I ever catch you flicking food again you'll be in real trouble." Leo turned to go back to his table but Mr

Peters' hand suddenly shot out and grabbed him by the collar. "We shall meet again this afternoon, shan't we?" Leo nodded. "Then another kindly word of warning — get your face scrubbed first, boy. I've seldom seen anyone quite as grimy as you." Leo nodded again and Mr Peters released him so that he was able to go back and sit down with the rest.

"He's right," said Fred, staring at Leo. "Your face is dirty."

"Shut up, Fred," said Maggie.

Leo turned to Marie. "Thanks," he said gratefully. "If it hadn't been for you he might have put me in detention or something." A horrified look spread across his face. "Crikey! He might have sent me to the head and you know what that means."

"Swish, swish, swish!" said Fred heavily and waved his arm up and down meaningly.

By this time everybody had finished eating and Mr Peters began sending them out into the playground table by table. He deliberately left theirs till last. Finally, when they were all sitting bolt upright and silent he nodded his head at them and they filed decorously past, only to hear the bell for the afternoon session go as soon as they were outside. "Old pig!" said Marie to Maggie, nodding in the direction of Mr Peters as he disappeared up the corridor.

Afternoon school seemed endless and they all sighed with relief when the bell rang at four o'clock. Maggie and Marie left arm in arm. "I'll go with you to pick up Bobby," Marie offered. "My mum won't mind if I'm late. She's gone off to see Aunt Pauline and if I do go home I'll only have to get Greg's tea. I don't know why everyone always thinks it's a girl's job. You wait till I'm married. It'll be a bit different then, I can tell you."

Maggie nodded in agreement. "It's funny, isn't it? It's just the same in our house. When we had Billy and Malcolm living at home it was always me who had to do the shopping and the washing-up and make the beds and help with Bobby. All they ever did was to want clean shirts and ask where their dinner was. They never lifted a finger. I get fed up being a girl sometimes."

"I don't," said Marie, as they squeezed past some women who were almost completely blocking the pavement. "I know it's rotten now but just you wait till we're a bit older." Her blue eyes glittered with anticipation. "I'm going to have every boy I know hopping around me all of the time. They won't know whether they're coming or going. I reckon that as long as you don't care about them you can have a smashing time for years and years."

They wriggled between a stall and a parked car and went round the corner that led to Bobby's school. A man came round it in such a hurry that he nearly banged into them. He looked startled and his narrow eyes shifted from one girl to the other. There was a momentary recognition as he stared at Maggie and then, with a curt kind of half-nod, he hurried off, his dirty fawn-coloured raincoat billowing out behind him.

"Who was that?" asked Marie idly.

"I don't know. I've never seen him before."

"I thought he knew you," persisted Marie.

Maggie shook her head so that her long dark hair flew about. "I've never seen him before," she said. "Anway he'd got that awful old cap pulled so low over his head that I didn't get a proper look at him."

"Neither did I. Still, he did look as if he knew you."

Maggie gave Marie a sudden push. "Come on. We'll be late for Bobby."

45

Marie gave a backward glance but the man had by now turned the corner, so she hurried up to join Maggie, who'd gone on ahead. "I still think he recognised you."

"Then he made a mistake," said Maggie in an uninterested way as she went into the infants' playground. She looked around. "Now where's Bobby got to? He's always standing at the gate. Don't tell me he's run off again."

"Coo-ee! Maggie! Maggie! I've got Bobby." The caretaker's wife was standing just inside the school entrance waving to them.

Maggie ran across. "Nothing's wrong, is there?" she asked anxiously. "Bobby's all right, isn't he? I mean, he's not hurt or anything?"

Mrs Buckle folded her arms across her overall and put down her broom. "No, he's all right," she said, "but I really can't make him out at all. He was standing by the gates waiting for you like he always does, although I wasn't watching him all the time, and then quite suddenly he came flying up to me crying and sobbing and holding on to my skirt, but he won't tell me what it's all about." She put her head round the corner of the door. "It's all right, Bobby," she said. "You can come out now. It's only Maggie come for you."

Bobby, his face tear-stained and slightly swollen, peered round the edge of the door, and then seeing Maggie he rushed across to her and started sniffling into her skirt.

Maggie bent down and put her arm round him protectively. "Now there's no need for all those tears," she said. "I'm here now. It's all right. There's nothing to cry about silly." She turned to the caretaker's wife. "Thanks ever so much Mrs Buckle. He won't do it again, will you Bobby?" Bobby only butted his head deeper into her skirt. "You are a little baby," she went on, her voice sounding slightly sterner.

"No one would think you're a big boy of five now the way you're carrying on. Here, blow your nose." She handed him her rather tattered handkerchief. He put it to his nose and gave a half-hearted snort and rubbed his eyes with the sleeve of his jersey.

"What's he got up his jumper this time?" asked Marie, noticing a large bulge round his stomach. Bobby immediately clutched at it.

Maggie felt the bulge. "It feels like that dirty old puppet. Why he doesn't just throw it away beats me. It's only fit for the dustbin." She glanced down at him and saw that his lower lip was trembling once again. "Oh, you might as well keep it for the time being, Bobby. Cheerio, Mrs Buckle, and thanks again."

"What was it all about, Bobby?" asked Marie as they left the playground. "Did some big kid hit you or did you fall over or something?" Bobby shook his head. "Did you think Maggie had forgotten you?" He shook his head again.

Marie turned to Maggie. "Honestly, anyone would think he was dumb or daft or something."

"He's a proper little chatterbox at home," said Maggie defensively. "Sometimes he nearly drives mum and me mad the way he carries on."

Marie looked at him doubtfully. "I suppose he has to give his tongue a rest sometimes then but it always seems to be when I'm around."

"Too much competition," said Maggie slyly.

Marie turned on her indignantly. "What do you mean by that?" she began truculantly, but then seeing Maggie was grinning she smiled too. They all three strolled along together until they reached the corner of Maggie's street and then just as they were saying goodbye, Bobby tugged at Marie's skirt.

"He tried to take it off me," he said in a tearful voice.

"Take what?" asked Marie.

"Who did?" demanded Maggie.

Bobby fumbled beneath his jersey and pulled out his puppet. "The man wanted it."

"Don't be so daft," said Maggie scornfully. "What on earth would a man want with a puppet, especially a tatty old thing like that? You're making it up." Bobby shook his head violently. "You mustn't go round telling stories."

"He did."

"Even if there was a man I expect he was only being nice to you. Come on, it's time I got you home. You sound tired to me." Waving goodbye to Marie, Maggie hurried off, tugging Bobby behind her.

Marie wandered slowly down the road by herself. She had no intention of going home to get tea for her brother. If he wanted it he could jolly well make it as far as she was concerned. She ambled along the Portobello Road, staring at the voiceless faces on the television screens in shop windows and stopping to admire her own reflection wherever she could see it. She stared critically at the clothes on display and mentally dressed herself in the best of them. She wondered how soon she could persuade her mother to let her have some higher heels. "She goes on and on thinking I'm a kid," she said to herself resentfully. "She'd really like to see me in white ankle socks with a pink bow in my hair." She looked down at her school skirt in disgust and counted up how many more years she still had to spend at school. The thought depressed her, so she crossed the road to the cinema. First she glanced at the stills of the week's film and then, almost unthinkingly, she ripped a bit more from the poster advertising an old horror film.

"And just what have you got against teenage werewolves?" hissed a voice in her ear and Marie swung round guiltily.

"I don't know what you mean," she began defensively, and then she smiled. "Oh, it's you, Joe. I didn't recognise you at first with that silly helmet on."

Joe looked offended. "It's my skid lid," he said. "It's a specially made egg-head skid lid, and not only that, it's the latest greatest model. Note the jagged flame on the front, track it round to the back," and he rotated solemnly round, "and what do you see?"

Marie examined the back of it. "A dragon," she said.

"That's my observant girl," he said appreciatively. "I am a dragon. No, to be exact, not just a dragon but one of *the* dragons, the Devastating Dragons, actually, the most dreaded mob in the whole of London."

"I've never heard of them," said Marie.

"Of course you haven't, my girl. It's a secret society and what's the use of a secret society if it isn't secret? And to tell the truth, it's very exclusive indeed. I only started it today."

"Who else belongs then?"

"It's exclusive, I told you. You don't think I'd let any of the great unwashed join, do you?"

"I think you're round the bend," said Marie simply but truthfully.

Actually Joe puzzled her and all of her friends. He didn't come from the Portobello Road but he had been around for some time and in spite of his accent and his exaggerated way of speaking and his extraordinary behaviour he had come to be accepted by most people. Whenever he was asked about his family or his background he told a totally different and quite improbable story each time. He always insisted that he was a lamplighter by profession, but since all the lamposts Marie had ever seen were electric, she didn't see how he ever had a job. His age puzzled her too. He sometimes looked as if he was only about seventeen, and at other times he seemed much older. It was funny, too, the way he sometimes had plenty of money and at others didn't seem to have a penny to his name. At the moment, however, he was clearly flush, since he had a new-looking motor scooter parked in the road.

He looked at her heavy satchel. "Haven't you been home yet?" he asked. "You must have changed since we last met. I always thought that you were last in school and first out. Perhaps, my dear Marie, you've been sitting at the feet of that handsome new art master, looking wide-eyed and innocent whilst planning yet another conquest. Perhaps I . . . "

"Gosh!" Marie put her hand to her mouth. "Maggie's got my English book and Mr Marsh'll go mad if I don't do his homework. I'll have to go all the way back to Maggie's. Lucky you mentioned school, Joe, or else I'd have completely forgotten about it."

Joe knelt at her feet, his hands clasped and raised in front of him. "Your devoted servant awaits your command, madam," he cried. "Order me where you will, even to the very ends of the earth, even into the jaws of death. Try me, fair lady!" and he flung his arms wide.

"You'll get your trousers dirty," said Marie prosaically, but secretly she was rather impressed by this performance.

Joe rose from the ground and brushed his trousers down. "Now you've stabbed me to the heart," he said reproachfully. "You've spurned me, tossed me aside like a rotten banana, left me a broken man. There's nothing now for me to live for," and he leaned up against the wall of the cinema and dabbed at his eyes with an oily rag.

"Now your face is all smutty," Marie pointed out.

Joe turned round, grasped her by the elbow and steered her over to the scooter. "There's no poetry in your soul, you vile girl. You probably haven't got a soul at all. I shall trample you in the dust the next time I pass by but in the meantime we'll go and get your English book. Now hop onto that," and he pushed her to the pillion of his scooter.

"What, on the scooter!" exclaimed Marie delightedly. "I've always wanted to go on one of those. Shall I hang on to your middle?"

"That's right, Cinders. Just put your sticky little paws round me and we'll be there 'ere the clock strikes twelve," and starting the engine he roared away down the street, Marie clinging tightly to him and hoping that some of her friends, or preferably enemies, would see her.

The minute they drew up outside Maggie's house Marie hopped off the scooter and rushed in and out within five minutes, waving the English book triumphantly in the air. Just as she was getting on again Joe turned and said to her, "Is that shifty character over there a friend of yours, Marie? I spotted him hanging around here the second we turned into the road and he's been lurking over there by the railings all the time you were in Maggie's house. He's standing under that tree pretending to be a branch right now."

Marie stared hard at him. "I'm not sure," she said slowly. "I mean, he's not a friend or anything, but he looks a bit like the bloke who nearly bumped into Maggie and me this afternoon. He looked at Maggie as if he knew her, but she said she'd never seen him before."

"He certainly seems interested in these houses, doesn't he?" said Joe thoughtfully. "And he hardly looks like an architectural student. I wonder what he's after."

"Lots of people just sort of hang around, don't they?" said Marie. "He doesn't actually have to be up to something. Perhaps he simply hasn't got anything to do."

"Do you think you'd know whether it was the same fellow or not if we managed to get a closer view?" asked Joe.

"I just don't know," said Marie. "I didn't really look at him. He is wearing the same sort of cap and the same sort of raincoat."

"So is half the population of London," murmured Joe. "Still let's go and see if we can stir him up a little," and he roared over to the man who, for all that he had pretended to be interested in the tree he was standing beneath, had been regarding them with an equal amount of interest.

"What do you want," he said belligerently as Joe skidded to a halt.

Joe let his eyes flicker up and down in an official sort of way. "Is your name John Smith?" he demanded.

"No it's not. What's it got to do with you anyway?"

"Never you mind," said Joe, fishing out a small black notebook from his pocket and flicking over the pages. He looked at his watch and made a note of the time at the top of the page. He then began writing laboriously in it. "He swore his name was not John Smith," he muttered as he wrote it down.

"What do you think you're playing at?" said the man truculantly. He turned his collar up and pulled his cap down.

"We'll come to that later," said Joe sharply. "I know your sort. You'll probably deny that you live in Buckingham Palace next."

"None of your business where I live. You're off your rocker, mate." By now the man not only looked uncomfortable but bewildered too.

Joe continued writing. "He was unwilling to give his name and address when asked and accused the officer of being mentally unsound." Joe handed the notebook to Marie. "Just sign that as a witness, will you? At the foot of the page will do." Marie obligingly scrawled her name. Joe shot one last piercing look at the man. "You'll be hearing from me again," he said, a hint of menace in his voice, as he started the engine. They zoomed off, leaving a totally baffled and disturbed man behind them.

Marie giggled so much that she might have fallen off the scooter had she not been clutching Joe so tightly. "Joe," she screamed into his ear, "didn't he look staggered? I reckon he really thought you were a copper."

"What do you mean by *thought?*" Joe shouted back. "I *am* a copper."

"Who do you think you're having on? Your hair's too long."

"Not for M.I.15, my little sugar plum," he yelled. "We are the silent but intrepid watchdogs of . . ."

"Oh, belt up! What do you take me for?" cried Marie, who hated to be taken for a fool.

Joe shrugged as they turned the corner into Marie's road and he drew up outside her house. "Very well, then," he said as they got off, "don't believe me — call me a liar if you will." He pulled out a large handkerchief and sobbed loudly into it.

"Come off it, Joe," said Marie, ringing the door bell.

Mrs Jenkins opened the door almost immediately. "A fine time to be coming home I must say," she began angrily but then, seeing Joe behind Marie, she went on in a reasonable tone, "but I dare say there's a good enough reason for it," and she smiled as pleasantly as she could.

Joe was a great favourite of hers. She couldn't exactly place him, but his accent impressed her and, as she frequently pointed out to Marie, you could tell he'd been nicely brought up. At the same time she was puzzled by his extraordinarily careless attitude to money and to convention generally. "Come on in, Joe," she said, "and have a cup of tea. The kettle's on the boil so it won't take a minute." Without waiting for an answer she led the way into the tiny, cold, bleak, front room that was only used on special occasions.

He poked his nose into it and shuddered. He looked at her reproachfully. "Mrs Jenkins," he said, "what have I done to deserve this? Are we friends no longer?"

Mrs Jenkins stood in the middle of the neat, chilly, little room and looked round anxiously. What on earth did he mean? She was proud of her front room and could see nothing wrong with it at all. "Whatever are you on about now, Joe?"

"That room," Joe said, poking his head a little further round the door and visibly shuddering, "is like a morgue — a beautifully furnished and spotless morgue, of course, and as morgues go, it's one of the most attractive I've ever seen — but since I'm still breathing I'd rather have my cuppa in the kitchen, if it's all the same to you," and he strode off down the passage to the kitchen with Mrs Jenkins hurrying after him.

"But it's nicer in there," she protested. "The kitchen's in a bit of a mess. I haven't had time to tidy it up."

"But I like your kitchen," said Joe, sinking down into the armchair. "It reminds me of home — all those delicious smells, the kettle singing on the hearth and cook in a vast white apron making cakes." He knew he couldn't fail with this sort of chat and he was quite right for Mrs Jenkins immediately bustled around with cups and saucers and plates.

"What on earth made you so late, Marie?" her mother asked as she poured tea into the teapot. "Greg had to get his own tea."

"Oh, I had to go back to Maggie's. I'd lent her a book I had to have and then I saw Joe on the way so he gave me a lift on his new scooter."

Mrs Jenkins looked very impressed. "So you've got a new scooter," she said as she brought him his tea in one of the best cups and placed a plate of biscuits by his elbow. "What made you get one of those?"

"It's really just a useful little runabout," drawled Joe, stretching out his long legs. "A Rolls is completely hopeless in London, you know. Parking's a bit of a headache these days."

"Must be," agreed Mrs Jenkins, nodding vehemently as though that was the only thing that prevented her having one too. "Aren't scooters a bit on the dangerous side though?"

Joe shook his head. "Not really, not if you've been practically brought up at Silverstone. To tell you the truth, it's a remarkably nippy little thing. It's handy in traffic and I really needed something for my job. Gas lamps are few and far between these days. You'd be surprised if you knew how much travelling I do. You see, there aren't really many of us left in the profession now. It's a dying art," and he sighed deeply and stirred his tea. Then, almost immediately, he brightened up again. He pointed a stabbing finger at Mrs Jenkins. "I've got it! You join the Gas Lamp Lighters' Union and come on my rounds with me and be initiated into the brotherhood. We could do with some new blood."

Mrs Jenkins was delighted at this bit of banter. She rubbed her hands up and down her apron and almost simpered. "Get along with you," she said.

Joe put down his cup and rose to his feet. "As a matter of fact, I must. Duty calls! Dusk falls!" He bent over Mrs Jenkins and raised her hand to his lips. "Thank you," he said. "Thank you for your hospitality." He blew a kiss to Marie. "So long, Mata Hari," he called, and then he disappeared through the front door.

"Now that's what I call a real gentleman," said Mrs Jenkins with satisfaction as she went into the scullery with the washing-up.

CHAPTER FOUR

"Did you see that bloke hanging round your house last night, Maggie?" asked Marie when they were waiting in the playground the next day after school.

"What bloke?" asked Maggie blankly. "I don't know what you're on about."

"The one Joe spotted when I popped in to get my English book last night. I told you Joe gave me a lift on his new scooter, didn't I?" Maggie nodded, a bored look on her face. That was all Marie had been able to talk about all day. "Well," Marie went on, "he spotted this bloke hanging about while I was inside and he just didn't like the look of him, so when I came out we gave him the fright of his life," and, giggling so much that she could hardly speak, she told Maggie all about it.

Maggie shook with laughter too. "Isn't Joe awful?" she said, hanging on to Marie's arm. "He hasn't half got a nerve, hasn't he?"

Gradually their giggles died down and Marie began looking back into the school impatiently. "Aren't the boys late? I'm getting properly fed up standing here. If they don't come soon I'm going to push off. I'm not waiting much longer."

Just then Alan and Fred came out together. "Where's

Leo?" Maggie asked. "Don't say we've got to wait for him now."

"We've been propping up the playground wall for so long now that I hardly dare leave it," said Marie. "It'll probably fall down without us."

"We've got to wait outside," said Alan. "Mr Marsh is coming. He's going to wait while Leo cleans up the playground. He got caught chucking a sweet paper on the ground, and you know what the head said."

"Leo!" exclaimed Marie incredulously. "Never! He never has any sweets except those we give him and none of us had any today. Gosh, he's a bit like a — a churchmouse — always hard up."

"No he's not," said Fred indignantly. "He's nothing like a mouse."

Marie ignored this as she led the way out of the playground. "Let's get out of here," she said. "Before we know where we are we'll be roped in as well. You know Mr Marsh." She turned to Alan. "Leo's a real nut, isn't he? Fancy letting himself get caught!"

"It wasn't his fault," said Fred as they went through the gates. "We had that student Miss Tilly . . . "

"Tolly not Tilly," said Marie irritably. "Can't you get anything right?"

". . . for drama," Fred went on, taking no notice of her, "and she said we never had any ideas of our own and she was going to make us use our imaginations."

"What did you use then?" muttered Marie.

Alan gave her a shove and a dirty look but Fred didn't even notice. "She said we'd all got to be in it," he went on, "and so she cleared a space in front of the class and she put a chair down and said that was the driver's seat and we'd all got to pretend it was a bus and get in the queue. It wasn't half daft. Some of us sat down in two lines behind the driver — that was Tom Dewson — and left a space down the middle and some of us had to stand. Anyway someone went 'ting ting' and we all started bouncing up and down and falling over each other and shouting at Tom and she kept on shouting at us but we couldn't hear what she was saying because of all the row. And then Tom yelled that he was pulling up because of the queue and they tried to get on and started climbing over the rest of us saying they were going upstairs. So then we had a fight."

"What happened then?" asked Maggie enviously. "We never have anything like that."

"Then Mr Marsh came in and said no games tomorrow and we'd all got to see the Head."

"What about Leo then?" asked Marie.

"He got caught in P.T. Tom gave him a sweet and he got caught throwing the paper away," explained Fred.

"What's it got to do with Miss Tolly and the drama lesson?" demanded Marie.

Fred stood absolutely still and thought hard for a few moments. "Nothing," he said at last.

"Pin-head!" snapped Marie. "You ought to get a medal. Pin-head of the week medal. You'd have a row of them in no time at all."

"Would I?" Fred looked vaguely pleased. He rather fancied the idea.

"Well, are we going to wait for Leo or not?" demanded Maggie.

"You'll be ever so late for Bobby," Alan pointed out.

"Mum's fetching Bobby tonight. She's going with Billy's wife to the clinic after because her baby's getting ever so fat."

"Is there anything wrong with him?" asked Alan.

"Course not. My mum wants them to see how well he's getting on. He can nearly walk now." Maggie looked round at them all proudly. She was the only one of them who was an aunt. "He can nearly walk now and he's only ten months."

"My mum says that I could walk when I was only eight months," said Marie complacently. "I could talk properly before I was a year too. Still, Maggie," she added condescendingly, "it's not bad for an ordinary kid."

"I suppose you were an extraordinary one," spat out Maggie.

Marie smiled. "Mm. The doctor says I was. He told my mum that he'd never seen a baby so far advanced and he'd been a doctor for years and years so he must have known."

"Why don't you shut up!" Maggie cried crossly. "We get fed up hearing you carry on about how marvellous you are. If you're as clever as you keep on saying you are what are you doing in my class? You ought to be at Eton or somewhere instead of in the Portobello."

"I bet the boys would like that," grinned Alan. "I can just see Marie dressed up in one of those Eton suits playing rugger."

Leo plodded wearily through the gates. "Cripes!" he said. "You aren't half a dirty lot dropping all that muck all over the playground. Five waste-paper baskets full I picked up."

"You're a fine one to talk," said Marie, picking a piece of silver paper out of his hair. "You're the one who was caught chucking sweet papers about, not us. We didn't have any."

"He only dropped one," said Fred.

"I bet that's because he didn't have any more to drop," said Alan.

"I don't know why I was the only one to be caught," said Leo resentfully. "I must have picked up about a thousand bits of paper and bottle tops and about a million paper darts.

They were all under 3A's window. I bet they had Miss Tolly, same as us."

"They did," said Alan. "I heard them."

Marie shifted from the wall. "I'm going home. I've had enough of this place. Anyone coming my way?"

"I will," said Alan. "I haven't got anything else to do except my homework."

"See you tomorrow," they said to the other three, and they strolled slowly along the Portobello Road. It was still reasonably busy although it was close to closing time. Marie gazed in shop windows as usual and Alan drifted along admiring some of the cars parked by the side of the road.

"Look at this," he said admiringly, coming to a halt beside a glittering new car. "It's the latest E-type. It's a lovely job, isn't it?"

Marie walked round it critically and then peered in. "I don't like the colour much," she said. "It doesn't go with the inside."

Alan waved his arms about in an effort to make her understand. "The colour doesn't matter. It's the car, the line, what's under the bonnet, that's what counts. This is a smashing piece of engineering. I bet it'll do eighty in third."

'Yes," said Marie in an abstracted way. She became more animated as she glanced in a shop window. "Look at those shoes, Alan! Aren't they a scream? Who on earth would buy shoes like that? They look as if they'd come straight out of the ark."

Alan looked up briefly from his examination of the Jaguar. "They look all right to me," he said. "They're just a pair of ordinary old shoes."

"Ordinary!" Marie was astonished at his lack of fashion sense. She tugged him nearer. "Look at them! You'd look a proper freak in those."

"You bet I would," said Alan.

Marie gave him a friendly shove so that he teetered on the edge of the gutter. They wandered along chattering to each other and calling out to the stall-holders they knew as they went past, stopping now and then to look at anything that caught their attention, reluctant to go home as long as the sun was shining. Suddenly, Marie grasped Alan's arm and pulled him behind a telephone box.

"What do . . . "

"Sh!" Marie carefully poked her head round the corner of the box for a moment. "Look!" she hissed, her voice hoarse with excitement. "There he is, over there."

Alan looked bewildered. "Who is? Who do you mean?"

"The man outside Maggie's last night."

"What man?"

"I told you," whispered Marie fiercely. "Oh, no I didn't. Well," and she embarked on the story once more. "And that's the man," she ended. "I know it is," and she pointed across the street.

"Which man is he?" hissed Alan. "The one outside Bobby's school or the one outside Maggie's house?"

"I'm positive he's the one outside Maggie's and he could easily be the same one as the one near the school." She poked her head round the corner once more. "What do you think he's doing, Alan?"

Alan took a cautious look. "He's looking at his watch."

"Clever! I've got eyes of my own, thank you very much. I can see he's looking at it, but what do you think he's doing here?" She clutched Alan's arm anxiously. "Gosh, he's coming over to me. What'll I do?" She half buried her head in Alan's blazer in an effort to avoid recognition.

As the man strode purposefully across the road Alan put

61

his arm slightly round Marie in a further effort at concealment. But the man walked straight past them and entered the telephone box and started dialling. Marie swivelled round so that her back was up against the back of the telephone box and Alan moved round too, so that he looked as if he was talking to Marie, but really so that he could stare straight at the man, who had now put down the receiver and was fumbling in his pocket for change. He thrust the money in the box. "That you, Graham?" he said loudly. "Harbottle here. Listen, I did what you . . . "

His voice tailed off as he turned sideways and leaned in a more comfortable position against the side. Alan stared at him. There really was nothing remarkable about him at all. His dark grey cap was pulled low on his forehead so that Alan could only see a few wisps of pale sandy hair sticking out. His eyes, set fairly well apart, were brown, and his skin was quite dark and slightly pitted. His lips were thin, and whenever he opened his mouth Alan could see strong-looking but dirty teeth. He looked a little shabby, but not unlike hundreds of men of his age.

However, Alan, who was not particularly sensitive, did get the feeling that in some way he might turn out to be a very nasty character if you happened to get on the wrong side of him. He could now hear very little of the conversation, but he was apparently having some sort of an argument with the man at the other end of the line. Just before he rang off he shouted so loudly that Alan could hear without making any effort at all. "All right," he snapped. "Call it child's play if you like, but let me tell you it's not all that easy. You ought to try it yourself." Then he listened for a moment or two more and said, "All right then, Graham. Yes, I heard you. O.K. Tomorrow." Then he banged the receiver down and pushed his way out of the telephone box clearly in an extremely bad temper. He elbowed a couple of passing girls who happened to be in the way and stamped off.

"It's O.K., Marie," said Alan. "He's just gone across the road again. He nearly knocked a couple of girls down in his hurry."

Marie lifted her head up. "Did he notice us?" she asked anxiously.

"No," said Alan. "Why should he? He probably only thought we were a couple of kids on their way home even if he did."

"Did you hear anything?" she asked eagerly. "I couldn't hear a word with my nose stuck in your blazer. You ought to have it cleaned. It stinks."

Alan disregarded this insult. "I did catch his name," he said, "and . . ."

"What's he called?"

"Harbottle."

"Harbottle! Harbottle! What a name. Fancy being called that," she exclaimed. "Mind you, it suits him. Well, what else did you hear?"

"I only caught the very end bit. He was telling this other man called Graham that he'd have to try again or something like that. It didn't really make much sense."

"None of it does really," admitted Marie, "but I'm positive that something funny's going on. It's queer the way he's always hanging around."

"He probably lives round here," Alan pointed out. "There's nothing funny in that."

"Then why haven't we seen him before?" she said sharply.

"Don't be so daft. We don't know everyone who lives round here."

"We do nearly." Her blue eyes sparkled and she began to bounce up and down excitedly. "Let's find out where he *does* live." She caught hold of his arm and tried to drag him along. "Let's follow him!"

Alan pulled back from her. "You must be off your rocker," he said.

"Why not!" Marie looked at his mulish expression. She knew how to get round him. "Oh, well," she said carelessly, "don't if you don't want to. I'm going anyway. He can't hurt me, not for just following him, if that's what you're afraid of."

"Who said I was afraid!" snapped Alan, his dignity hurt. "It just seems a bit pointless, that's all. Still if you want to . . ."

"Let's run," said Marie, grinning at him now that she'd got her own way. "We might lose sight of him if we don't get a move on."

Together they rushed down the road, weaving in and out of mothers and push-chairs and wandering children until they drew level with their quarry, who was still on the other side of the road. "It's a good thing there are still plenty of people about," panted Alan, "or he couldn't help noticing us." As he dodged between two women with dogs on leads, one of the dogs made a dive for something in the gutter and Alan stumbled into a woman who was wheeling a pram piled high with shopping. A bulging string bag on the top of the pram wobbled for a moment and then fell, disgorging a torrent of onions, potatoes, peas and carrots that cascaded all over the pavement. The baby in the pram, previously obscured by shopping, woke up and began wailing loudly. "Why don't you kids look where you're going?" said the woman loudly. "Taking up the pavement like that. Anyone would think you owned it. Look what you've done!"

Marie took no notice and hurried on, but then she suddenly realized that Alan was no longer by her side. She looked back. Red with embarrassment, he was on his knees stuffing the vegetables back into the string bag. "Potty," she said to herself. But she went back and held the mouth of the bag open so that he could push the things back more easily.

"Thanks," said the woman, grudgingly, "but just you watch where you're going next time."

Marie grabbed Alan and dragged him away. "Miserable old cat. It was just as much her fault as yours. It wasn't your job to stuff her rotten old carrots back in her bag. It would have served her right if she'd had to do it herself. She didn't look where she was going."

Alan hardly noticed what she was saying. He stopped trotting and looked around. "Now we've lost him," he said. "I can't see him anywhere."

Marie stopped and stared around. She looked up and down the road. Alan was right. He was no longer in sight. Furiously she turned on Alan. "It's all your fault," she cried. "You're so busy doing things for people you don't even know you don't notice if you let your friends down — and if you did notice, I don't suppose you'd care. You'll get backache if you go on bowing and scraping to people. If Fred's pin-head of the year, then you're boot-licker of the year. You're just about the end!"

She glanced hopelessly around once more and then just as she did so, she saw their quarry emerge from a tobacconist's. Her face brightened immediately. "There he is," she said. "That's him coming out. Come on!" Once more she tugged at Alan, but this time he was as unyielding as a poker. "We'll lose him again," she said impatiently. She looked up at his stiff face. "What's up, Alan?" she asked, genuinely surprised at his unresponsiveness.

"You'd better follow him on your own. I'm going to be too busy licking boots."

"Oh, Alan," said Marie, "I didn't mean it. You know I didn't." She tried to sound contrite, but the truth was she was seldom sorry for anything she did. "Please, Alan, it won't be the same without you — and . . ." she tried to look nervous, " . . . he looks as if he could turn nasty." She fidgeted with a button on his coat. "I mean, I'm not exactly scared but . . ." and she let the sentence die away knowing only too well how flattered Alan would be at her apparent dependence on him.

"Oh, well, all right then," said Alan, trying not to sound too eager. He was delighted that Marie should admit that she needed him, but then he added, "but you'd better watch what you say in future. I shan't give you a second chance."

Marie hardly bothered to listen to him once she knew she'd won. Her eyes were firmly fixed on the cloth cap now jogging down the road. "He's turned into Latimer Road," she said and together they scuttled round the corner after him. "I wonder if he's going on the tube."

"We'll have had it if he does," remarked Alan. "I'm skint."

Marie felt in her pockets, although she already knew it was a fruitless search. "So am I," she admitted.

The man went round the corner into Ladbroke Grove and, as they looked cautiously before turning into it themselves, they saw him go straight into a cafe. Marie pushed her nose up against the steamy window. "He's got a cup of tea and a cheese roll," she said, "and now he's got his football pools out. Gosh!" she said in a disgusted tone, "if he's going to do those we could be here all night."

"Come away from the window," hissed Alan. "He's coming out again." They rushed into a nearby doorway and stood there hardly daring to breathe as he clomped by. He went straight over to the newspaper seller.

"Evening, Tom," he said as he took one.

"Lovely evening, isn't it? Hope you backed a winner."

Harbottle, his newspaper now open at the racing results, strolled back to the cafe again and sat down.

Marie nudged Alan. "That was a lucky escape," she said. "All we've got to do now is to find out where he lives." Her face fell. "We could be here for hours though, waiting for him to come out. I wish I could think of something."

Alan stood there silently for a minute or two. "I've got an idea," he said at last. "Just wait for me. This might work." He pulled out an envelope addressed to himself and walked over to the newspaper man. They had a brief conversation and Alan came back looking very pleased with himself.

"Well," said Marie eagerly. "What did you find out?"

"Where he lives, of course."

"Oh, Alan, you are clever," she cried and Alan almost smirked at the flattery.

"It was easy enough," he said, trying to sound modest. "I said we thought the man who'd just bought the paper had dropped the envelope but we weren't sure and didn't like to bother him. The newspaper bloke looked at it and he said it couldn't be his because it wasn't his name and anyway he lived in East Westbourne Mews. So there you are," he finished triumphantly. "We've got his name *and* address."

Marie flung her arms round him. "Honestly, you're marvellous, Alan! That really was brilliant! Now we can watch him any time we want. I've been past those mews lots of times. There are only about ten houses. It ought to be easy enough to find out which one. Oh, it's super!"

Alan, feeling slightly embarrassed and in agonies in case any of his friends should see him, detached her arms and stepped back. A slight frown creased his forehead. "I don't know what good it'll do," he said doubtfully. "I mean, we can't exactly put a twenty-four hour watch on his house, can we?"

Marie looked at him indignantly. She put her hands on her hips and frowned back. "Of course it'll do some good," she said flatly. "I know we can't watch him all of the time but if we want to know anything specially we know where to look for him."

Alan regarded her sceptically. It seemed to him that Marie was becoming obsessed by the whole thing and anyway, he didn't care for dramatics. "I can't quite see why we want to watch him," he said. "For all we know he's just an ordinary guy who lives round here. When you come down to it you only think he's suspicious because you've bumped into him twice in one day. You can hardly call that evidence, can you?"

"But Joe thought he was fishy too!" cried Marie.

"Oh, well, you know Joe. I expect he was just in a cops and robbers mood. I don't suppose that means anything at all."

"Oh, clear off then if that's the way you feel," shouted Marie, childishly stamping her foot. "I'll manage on my own, thank you very much. In fact I'll probably get on better without you," and she turned her back on him and stared into the cafe once again.

Alan hesitated for a moment. He didn't like the idea of leaving her on her own and when Marie was in this sort of mood he usually tried to get her out of it. He knew that she seldom meant half of the things she said, but on the other hand he was getting hungry and he was also a bit fed up with the way she was carrying on. Perhaps it would do her good, he reasoned, to find that she couldn't always have her own way.

"All right then," he said finally. "You stay here and play your own little game. I'll leave you to it, since that's what you seem to want." He walked away without a backward glance and, threading his way through the crowds coming out of the underground station, was soon completely out of sight.

Abandoned on the pavement, Marie began to wish that she had been a little more diplomatic. Although she'd said she'd track Harbottle alone, she wasn't too keen on the idea of being on her own. It was just beginning to get dark and the crowd of shoppers and people returning from work was gradually beginning to disperse. Still, she wasn't going to admit to Alan the next morning that she hadn't dared to follow Harbottle, so she settled down behind a pile of crates in a side alley that gave her a reasonable view of the cafe, grimly prepared to wait until midnight if necessary. She was hoping that Harbottle would go straight home, so that she would be able to look at Alan in the morning with a superior little smile and be able to say casually, "Oh, by the way, he lives at number four," or whatever it was. Hugging her knees, which were beginning to get a little cold, for a warm spring day soon changes to a chilly spring evening, Marie practised the smile and the airy little laugh which would accompany it.

"Well, what are you doing down there, young lady?" Marie looked up from her reverie to find a large policeman looming over her. He looked ostentatiously at his watch. "Don't you think you'd better be running along home? It's getting late, you know."

Marie, her face pink, brushed some of the long fair strands of hair away from her face and then scrambled to her feet. "I was just going," she mumbled and began to walk towards the cafe, feeling that the policeman's eyes were following her all the time, so that she couldn't stop or even dawdle past it. Fate was on her side. Just before she reached the cafe the door swung open and Harbottle himself hurried out without even a glance in her direction and started off up the street.

Eagerly Marie half-walked and half-ran after him, for he was moving along at a very swift pace. He strode along, looking neither to the right or the left and then, glancing at his watch, he broke into a trot and crossed the road, dodging in and out of the traffic. Marie panted after him and, seeing a gap in the almost endless stream of lorries, cars and vans, plunged recklessly across after him only to be left marooned on an island as he gained the safety of the other side. She bit her lip angrily as a bus rolled up to the stop and Harbottle just managed to leap onto it as the conductor rang the bell.

"Just my luck," Marie muttered crossly to herself. "All that hanging around for nothing. I've wasted hours. I bet Alan won't believe me. He'll think I just gave up. Oh, it's just not fair." In spite of all this grumbling to herself Marie was perhaps secretly rather relieved for although it had been a lovely day it was getting chilly and she was only wearing her school skirt and blouse. What was more, although she would rather have died than admit it, the idea of being in a strange neighbourhood on her own at this time in the evening really didn't appeal any more.

It was quite a long way home and Marie was already tired and so she dragged back, occasionally kicking at anything that happened to be in her path. Every now and then a motor scooter puttered past and she looked up hopefully in case it was Joe, and each time she was disappointed. Eventually she turned wearily into her street and then she felt a great sinking feeling in the pit of her stomach as she saw her mother hanging over the gate and looking anxiously up and down the road.

Mrs Jenkins' worried look changed to one of relief as she saw Marie approaching, but it was replaced almost immediately by one of anger. "You are a naughty girl, Marie!" she exclaimed, as soon as Marie was within hearing distance. "I've been worried out of my mind. Where were you? You know I won't have you coming home late. Who were you with? What were you up to? I've been running in and out of the house every two minutes and worrying myself sick. Anything might have happened to you. You might have been run over or run away with or anything — though anyone running away with you would find he'd bitten off more than he could chew. You're more trouble than you're worth."

She seized Marie's shoulders and shook her so hard that her hair tumbled all over her face. She went on, her voice getting shriller and shriller. "Don't you ever dare stay out late again or I'll really give you something to remember. Now just you get inside the house before I properly lose my temper." She gave Marie a push that sent her stumbling towards the front door.

"Oh, come off it, Mum," Marie said wearily.

Her mother gave her another push towards the kitchen. "Don't you speak to me like that, young lady," she cried, infuriated by Marie's off-hand manner. "You remember who you're talking to. I'm not one of your guttersnipe friends, so you watch what you say. Any more of that sort of talk and I'll see that you don't go out at all. That'll soon stop you picking up their disgusting manners and talk. I've never heard anything like it!" and she stood over Marie quivering with anger.

Marie kicked off her shoes and slumped into a chair. She felt absolutely exhausted. "All right, Mum," she said, "I'm sorry. Don't go on at me."

Her mother gave her a sharp look. She folded her arms and stood before Marie looking grimly at her. "I want to know where you were, who you were with and exactly what you were doing," she said.

"Sh!" said Marie, trying to give herself time to think.

71

"You're shouting. What'll the neighbours think?"

Mrs Jenkins cast an anxious look at the walls as if they might suddenly sprout ears. "Well, come on, out with it. I want the truth, mind," but although the words were still belligerent, her voice was quieter.

Marie closed her eyes for a second and flogged her tired brain. The last thing she could possibly do was to tell the truth. "I had to help one of the teachers," she said quickly, knowing that this would be well received.

"At this time of night?" said her mother, a suspicious look on her face. "What was so important that it couldn't wait till morning?"

"It was about the play we're doing in school." Marie said quickly, looking back at her mother with wide-open, candid eyes. She couldn't really remember much about it since neither she nor her friends were in it. It was only when Ann Lucas was called out of class for rehearsals that she was reminded that there was going to be one at all.

"What play? You haven't said anything about it before."

"Yes I have," said Marie untruthfully, "but you were so busy giving Greg his tea that you didn't really listen to me." She switched a hurt expression onto her face.

"What's it about then?"

"Oh, well, it's about a princess and all that," said Marie vaguely. "Miss Fisher wanted to talk about clothes and scenery and things."

This sounded perfectly reasonable to Mrs Jenkins, who thought it only natural that Marie's advice should be needed. "Well, I don't mind so much if you were with a teacher," she said, "but I really don't think it right to keep a young girl like you out so late without letting her mother know. I've a good mind to write your Miss Fisher a note."

Alarmed, Marie sat bolt upright. "You'd just look like a

proper fusspot, Mum. I bet Alan's mother won't write a note. She'll just be pleased that me and Alan were chosen. Everybody wanted to stay but we got picked because Miss Fisher said we were the most reliable."

A self-satisfied smile flitted across her mother's thin face. "So she chose you and Alan," she repeated smugly. "Well, I can't say I'm surprised. Although I say it myself, and I'm not one to boast, there's no doubt about it she did pick two nicely brought-up children. I notice she didn't pick Maggie and that Leo. Not that I've got anything against them. After all, Maggie's mother does her best, and it isn't Leo's fault that he hasn't got a mother — but it just shows what I've always said, it pays to be nicely mannered. People do notice, especially teachers. Now Alan's always struck me as a thoroughly nice boy, and his mother keeps the house a treat. Now that's a place where you really could eat off the kitchen floor and you can't say that about many houses these days." She looked smugly at her own highly-polished linoleum.

Marie hardly listened to this self-congratulatory stream of chatter. She found it difficult enough just to keep her eyes open. She felt only a sense of relief at preventing her mother from writing a note, for if she had she would have expected an answer and then the fat really would have been in the fire. At last Mrs Jenkins stopped talking and disappeared into the scullery. She soon returned with a plate of bacon and eggs and a large pot of tea.

"I'm not sure you deserve it," she said, putting them down, "but I suppose it really wasn't your fault if you were helping Miss Fisher. Eat it up while it's hot, there's a good girl."

Marie wolfed the food down, accompanied by a series of reproachful remarks. "Not so much in your mouth at once, Marie." "Don't use your knife like a shovel, Marie." "I'm

73

glad Miss Fisher can't see you now, Marie." However, she was much too tired to care, and certainly hadn't the energy to answer back. She finished the food and pushed the plate away.

"Now go and get ready for bed. Don't forget to clean your teeth. Put on your dressing-gown and do your homework upstairs where it's nice and quiet."

Marie climbed the stairs slowly and, ignoring both her teeth and her homework, crept into bed. "What a day!" she thought, and dropped off to sleep.

CHAPTER FIVE

The following morning Mr Marsh had the class busily but unenthusiastically writing an essay called "A Day in the Country", but since few of them ever went to the country, and only caught occasional glimpses of it on their way to the seaside, they found it particularly difficult to do.

Marie sucked the end of her pen and mentally composed the opening sentence of the confidential chat she meant to have with Alan during break. She had been so late for school that she hadn't had time to talk to anyone. At first she had rather liked the idea of "At Trafalgar Square he still hadn't cottoned on to the fact that he was being trailed" — but then she realised that simply wouldn't do, since Alan knew she hadn't had a penny on her. "As soon as I spotted the plain-clothes man I knew I'd better leave it to him" sounded dramatic enough, but also hopelessly unlikely. She turned them over in her mind. If they didn't sound convincing to her then they wouldn't fool Alan for a moment. She sucked her pen a bit harder.

"Marie!" She glanced up and saw Mr Marsh looking at her with a weary expression on his face. "All you've done for the last five minutes is nibble your pen. Do get on with your work for a change."

Marie bent her head down and tried to look busy while the rest of the class, which had up to then been quiet, stirred restlessly. There was a tap on the classroom door and a boy walked in with a note for Mr Marsh. Everyone looked up, glad of the interruption. Mr Marsh ran his eyes over it. "Margaret Hobbs," he said, "Miss Fisher wants to see you in her room. You'd better go straight away."

They all turned round and stared at Maggie, who looked both startled and apprehensive. She closed her books slowly and edged her way between the desks and past Marie. "What's up?" hissed Marie. Maggie shrugged her shoulders and made an I-don't-know face at her.

"Marie!" snapped Mr Marsh. "I've already told you to get on with your work. If you haven't done enough to satisfy me you'll have to stay in at break. You really will have to learn to mind your own business."

Several girls sniggered and a number of heads turned to look at her. Marie flushed and lowered her head once again and tried to think of another sentence to write. Why couldn't he give them more interesting subjects to write about, she thought. "Why I hate teachers" for instance, or "What I've got against school". She could say plenty about those. She dragged her mind back to the day in the country and looked at it despairingly. What a lot of old rubbish she'd written! Oh, well, she thought, and wrote a few more uninspired lines. Mr Marsh, strolling past, looked at her book in a disapproving way but said nothing.

Just as the bell went, Maggie bounced back into the classroom, looking very sparkly and happy. Mr Marsh had the books passed to the front and then, just before he left the room, he told Marie to pick them up and take them to the staff room for him. She made a hideous face at his back but when he turned round she was wearing a demure and innocent expression.

When she finally got out into the playground she found a large, excited, chattering group round Maggie. "What's going on?" she asked, pushing her way to Maggie's side.

Maggie turned a flushed and excited face on her. "You'll never guess," she said, "not in a thousand years."

"What?"

"Go on, guess," urged Maggie.

"We haven't got a thousand years," Marie pointed out. "We've only got about ten minutes so you might as well tell me."

"Well," began Maggie, "did you notice that Ann Lucas is away?" Marie shook her head. She wasn't interested in Ann Lucas. "Well," Maggie continued, "she kept saying she had a headache . . ."

"Get a move on, Maggie," said Marie, anxious to get the story over so that she could embark on her own with everyone paying the proper amount of attention.

"I would if you'd only stop interrupting me," said Maggie. "As I said she'd got a headache and kept saying she felt funny yesterday and they've found out she's got chicken-pox, so Miss Fisher's asked me to take her part!"

"You!" Marie was staggered. Why Maggie? Why not her?

"What part?" asked Fred as he joined the group with Leo.

"The princess!" answered someone.

A puzzled frown creased Fred's forehead. "Are you twins then?" he asked.

"Oh, Fred!"

"Do you mean in the play?" asked Leo, looking impressed. "Crikey! That's the chief part. I bet you'll be ever so good, Maggie. I've always thought you were the best actress in the school."

77

"Second best," said Marie meanly. "If she'd been the best she'd have been chosen first instead of Ann Lucas."

Marie was feeling jealous. She looked much more like a princess than Maggie, she knew she did. Hadn't she got long fair hair and blue eyes, whereas Maggie had ordinary old brown hair and eyes? Of course she had. Wasn't she taller and more graceful, and prettier? She knew she was. Everybody said so. Then why had Maggie been picked? It must have been favouritism, she decided. It couldn't have been anything else. It just wasn't fair. "I suppose you'll fit the costume," she said casually. "You're the same size as Ann Lucas. I suppose it was cheaper than getting a new one."

Leo looked at her in disgust. "Aren't you mean!" he said.

"She's jealous," said Fred ponderously. Marie jabbed him in the ribs and scowled at them both.

Maggie hadn't really heard what Marie had said. "Gosh!" she rattled on enthusiastically. "Isn't it smashing! I'm going to have a crown in my hair or a coronet or something and I'm going to have the long white dress Ann Lucas's mother made and . . ."

"See!" sneered Marie.

". . . not much time so I've got to try and learn most of the words tonight. I'll have to go home early. Marie, could you do me a favour and pick up Bobby?"

"No I can't," snapped Marie. "Even if you are a princess I'm not your slave." She saw that everyone was looking at her disapprovingly and so she added hastily, "Actually I've got something I've just got to do tonight. It's terribly important otherwise I would."

Maggie's face fell. "I'll go, Maggie," offered Leo. "He's used to me. He won't mind."

"So will I," said Fred.

"Oh, super! You're really smashing!" said Maggie. "I'll do the same for you sometime."

"We haven't got any little brothers," said Fred.

Out of the corner of her eye Marie saw Alan approaching. She waved her hand in the air to catch his attention. "By the way, Alan," she began importantly, "I thought you might like to know that after you'd gone I trailed . . ."

"Maggie's going to be the princess!" Fred shouted. "She'll be fabbo, won't she?"

Alan patted Maggie on the head. "Super," he said. "I thought what a good actress you were last Christmas when we did that play. I don't know why Miss Fisher didn't choose you right away."

Marie took a deep and angry breath. She looked furiously at Alan who was smiling down at Maggie. He hadn't even noticed her, let alone listened to her. All his attention was focused on Maggie. "There's a song to sing too," she said, "and I told Miss Fisher that I wasn't very good at singing but she said she thought I had quite a pretty voice even though it wasn't very strong."

Marie planted herself squarely in front of Alan. "You know that man," she said, "the one we were track . . ."

Alan moved round so that he was facing Maggie again. "You won't have a lot of time to learn your part," he said warningly. "Aren't they doing the play the Saturday after next?" Maggie nodded. "I'll tell you what," he said. "Shall I come round and hear your lines? It's easier if there are two. I'll come round at any old time. You've only got to say the word."

Marie edged Maggie out of the way once more. "Once when he thought he . . ." she began, but Alan moved round her once again so that he could talk directly to Maggie.

"When's your first rehearsal?" Leo asked. "If it's after

school I'll look after Bobby until your mum comes home."

"Everyone else has been rehearsing for about a fortnight," Maggie said, "but Miss Fisher said she'd take me on her own as much as she could. I'm being let off lessons for the rest of the morning and she's going to have me for a little bit this afternoon."

Marie made one last despairing attempt to gain everyone's attention. "And when he pulled this gun out," she said wildly, "he . . ."

"The dragon's head is being made by Mr Donaldson . . ."

"The police said I was . . ."

". . . is doing the scenery."

". . . bodies and blood all over the road!" Marie shouted. She looked at the eager faces turned towards Maggie. It was no use. They hadn't heard a word she'd said. She stamped off, defeated. Standing on her own by the wall she sulkily watched the crowd round Maggie growing larger and larger. "If they don't need me then I can do without them," she muttered to herself.

Eventually Fred came over to her, a wide grin on his face. "Isn't it all super!" he said happily. He looked at Marie's sullen scowl. "What's wrong with you then? Get out of the wrong side of your bed, did you?"

"Oh, clear off," she snapped irritably. "Go back to the fan club. I don't need you or anybody else."

"All right," said Fred amiably and ambled back to the others. Marie stood there miserably on her own until, much to her relief, the bell went.

All through the rest of the day Marie watched resentfully as Maggie drifted to and from classes, happily unaware of Marie's smouldering anger. Marie began to feel isolated, ignored by everyone, friends and enemies alike. She might have realised, had she thought about it, that her glowering face would have put anyone off speaking to her, but it didn't even occur to her and so she just became more and more furious with everyone. As the last bell went and the class began packing their cases and satchels, Maggie made her way across to Marie and for the first time noticed her furious face.

"What's wrong, Marie?" she asked sympathetically.

"There's nothing wrong with *me*," said Marie meaningly. "I haven't got a swollen head even if somebody else has." She swept her books into her bag and pushed past Maggie and rushed into the corridor, where she bumped into Alan who was hurrying into their classroom. "Alan," she said eagerly. "You're just the person I wanted to see. What time shall we meet this evening? I've got a fantastic amount to tell you."

Alan was taken aback. He couldn't think what she was talking about. "I'm going over to Maggie's," he said. "I thought you knew."

"But Alan," Marie said, sounding reproachful, "you promised. You know you did."

"No I didn't," said Alan. "I didn't promise anything of the sort."

Marie looked up and fluttered her eyelids at him. That usually worked on Alan. "Well, maybe you didn't exactly promise," she admitted, "but I did think that after yesterday it was sort of understood we'd . . ."

"What about tomorrow?" said Alan, anxious to join Maggie. "We could talk about it then, that's if Maggie doesn't need me. We'll fix something up." He brushed past her and went on into the classroom leaving Marie, for once utterly speechless, alone in the corridor.

Leo and Fred emerged from their classroom and went past Marie. "We're going to get Bobby," Leo shouted to her. "Going to come with us, Marie?"

"Sorry, Nanny," she said cuttingly. "I've got other fish to

fry. You'll just have to go walkies on your own." She looked sharply at them, hoping to have provoked some reaction to what she imagined were really cutting remarks, but they went on, jabbering away to each other as if the words hadn't even penetrated. Marie herself hadn't any real idea of what she wanted to do but she hurried after them and deliberately shoved each of them into the wall as she overtook them and rushed along importantly without even a backward glance.

Leo and Fred met each other's eye. "I wonder what's up with her?" Leo said as he rubbed his elbow.

"Just ordinary old bad temper," said Fred placidly. "It runs in the family. Look at her mother. She's just the same. I bet that's why her dad stays in the navy."

"Her mum's all right really," said Leo, happy memories of a good meal in the forefront of his mind. "Her bark's worse than her bite. Mind you, I bet living with Marie makes her worse than she is. She'd make it tough for a saint to stay saintly I reckon. What really gets me about her is the way she's always sarcastic."

Fred opened his eyes in surprise. "Sarcastic? Marie? I hadn't noticed. Hey! Listen! Is that Bobby crying?"

They broke into a trot and followed the noise round the corner to the infant's school. Bobby was standing just inside the gates of the playground holding on tightly to his puppet. His mouth was wide open and he was screaming loudly. Several women were standing by watching. Close to him just outside the school was a dark-haired man of about forty who was crouching down so that his head was on a level with Bobby's. He seemed remarkably well-dressed and respectable-looking. He was talking earnestly to Bobby and waving his horn-rimmed glasses about as if to emphasise the points he was making. But Bobby was howling so loudly that it was doubtful whether he could possibly have heard a word of what the man was saying. As the man heard the sound of racing footsteps and looked up and saw Leo and Fred pounding along, a quick expression of annoyance flashed across his face and was immediately replaced by one of amused despair. "You'll be able to buy two of them," he was saying persuasively as Fred and Leo pounded up. "They'll be clean and new and you'll be able to move their arms and legs about."

As Leo reached Bobby and bent down to him, the small crowd dispersed. "What's up?" he asked.

Mrs Buckle appeared from round the corner of the playground. "I've been keeping an eye on him," she said, "all the time this gentleman was talking to him. He hasn't done anything to him but talk. Ah well, I've got my work to do." She picked up her bucket and moved away.

"What do you want to make him cry for?" asked Leo aggressively. "Leave him alone, can't you? Come on Bobby we're taking you home tonight. Maggie's busy," and he took hold of Bobby's hand. At this Bobby stopped wailing and started sobbing instead. Fred took hold of the hand with the puppet in it and the three of them began to walk away together.

The man stood up and strolled alongside them. "I really haven't done the young man any harm," he said pleasantly. "That lady, the one in the school yard, would confirm that I merely spoke to him."

"He doesn't want to talk to you," said Leo firmly.

"You've got it all wrong, you know. I was, I think, offering your young friend a bargain."

"He doesn't want any bargains from you. Can't you see how you've upset him. Why don't you clear off and leave him alone?"

"I rather believe he was crying because the lady with the

bucket insisted that he stayed within the school precincts and not because of anything I said at all."

Fred and Leo took a tighter grip on Bobby's hands and hurried him along even faster so that his legs hardly had time to touch the ground, but the man nevertheless kept pace with them. Fred turned to him. "Why don't you hop it, mister? Hark at him! He's still bawling and it's all your fault."

The man laughed in a good-natured way, showing extremely even and white teeth. "Goodness, what an ogre you seem to think I am. Actually I'm a collector. I collect old puppets and dolls as a matter of fact. Of course, I haven't a particularly large collection as these things go, but although I say it myself, it is rather a good one."

Fred gave him a queer look and slackened his pace a little. "That's a funny thing to do, isn't it?" he remarked slowly. "I mean it's funny since you're not a girl, and anyway most girls give up dolls when they get older."

"I suppose it is a strange hobby," the man admitted with a smile. "I've never really thought about it before but then people do do odd things, don't they? After all, there are male dress designers — the best of them are men, as a matter of fact — male ballet dancers, male chefs, the list is endless actually. Besides, silly though it may sound to you, my hobby does have some little importance of its own, historically speaking, that is."

Fred's face was by now a little less suspicious but Leo was still regarding him dubiously. "Still," said Fred, harking back to the man's greatest crime, "it was you who made Bobby cry and he hasn't stopped properly yet and I don't suppose he will till you've gone, so you'd better go."

"I hardly regard myself as guilty but perhaps you're right. I might have been my fault but I do feel that the caretaker had just a little to do with it."

"Bobby likes *her*," Leo said meaningly.

"Then of course I shall go," he said, "but perhaps you'd be good enough just to explain the offer I was making to him. I'm not really good with small children and you probably know the right way to handle them." He looked directly at Fred as he spoke. At this Fred felt extraordinarily pleased. Hardly anyone ever thought he was good at anything. "You see," continued the man, "that rather tatty old puppet that he's grasping so firmly is of some interest to me. I have had a quick squint at it, and although it really is in a rather dreadful condition, it's fairly old and I haven't seen one like it before so I thought I'd like to make the young man an offer for it."

Leo looked up and shook his long thick hair out of his eyes. "How much?" he said quickly.

"I thought a couple of guineas would be fair."

Fred was very impressed at hearing someone actually talking about guineas. Up till then he'd thought they only existed in arithmetic books. "Well, could he get another one for that?"

The man looked amused. "He could get a couple of glove puppets or he could put it towards a string puppet if he'd rather."

"Cripes!" said Fred. He bent down. "Did you hear that, Bobby? If you give that man your dirty old puppet you can have two nice new ones."

Bobby stopped sniffling. He cuddled the puppet. He shook his head and stuck out his lower lip stubbornly. "No!" he said vehemently. "It's mine!"

Fred looked shocked. He couldn't bear to see Bobby turning down such a marvellous opportunity. He simply couldn't understand it. "You're barmy, Bobby. Look at its nose. It's all broken and it's hair's filthy. It stinks. I'd do

85

what the gentleman wants and get two lovely new ones instead, that's what I'd do. Look, he's got the money in his hand all ready," and indeed, as if by magic, two crisp pound notes and two bright coins were waved under Bobby's nose

Bobby looked at the money and then at the puppet. "Mine!" he said firmly, and he stroked the puppet's stringy hair lovingly. Then he looked up hopefully at Leo and said, "Ice-lolly, Leo?"

The stranger roared with laughter. "Aha! I see it now. The little fellow's blackmailing me." He put his hand into his pocket and pulled out some change. "Perhaps you'd be good enough," he said to Fred, "to pop along to that shop and buy him one. You might as well buy three of the revolting things while you're about it. I'm sure that you and your friend could do with one as well."

"Not for me," said Leo.

As soon as Fred had gone the man turned to Leo. "To tell you the truth," he said pleasantly, "I must say that I do have a slight twinge of guilt about this, but only a twinge, you understand. I'm quite sure that Bobby will get far more pleasure out of a new one, and I'm equally sure that his mother won't put up with a dreadful old thing like that in her house for very long, so in a sense I might really be doing him a slight favour. Actually it really was a stroke of luck my seeing him there, just standing with it. I really don't have anything quite like it in my collection although I do have several similar ones. They were quite common about a hundred years ago when most toys were made of wood but they're becoming rarer year by year."

Fred came back with the ice-lollies and the change. He tore the paper wrapping off Bobby's and started licking his own. "Thanks," he said. Then he looked down reprovingly at Bobby. "You didn't say thank you to the nice man, Bobby.

Say thank you properly." Bobby shook his head violently and crunched away hastily just in case it was going to be taken from him.

Fred was quite upset at this display of bad manners. "It's rude not to say thank you, Bobby. Go on, say it."

Bobby crammed the last of the lolly into his mouth and threw the stick away. "No!" he said distinctly.

Fred looked shocked and cuffed him round the head. "Oh, you are naughty," he said. "Naughty and rude, that's what you are."

"Never mind," said the man. "It really doesn't matter." He bent down once more and crackled the notes invitingly and clinked the money loudly. "Now what about our little deal, young man?"

Bobby looked up at Leo's expressionless face and then he looked hard at Fred's beaming, encouraging one and then he gazed at the money. With absolute finality he shook his head.

"I'll tell you what, I'll make it three guineas. How about that?" The man smiled up at the boys. "He's driving a hard bargain but I must confess I'm really getting quite keen on it." He put his hand first into his breast pocket and then dived into his trouser pocket and showed Bobby the extra money. "Well," he said easily, "what about that?"

Bobby just cuddled the puppet a little closer and turned his back on the man. He began to sing the puppet a song. The man raised his eyebrows humorously at the boys and moved round so that he was facing Bobby once more. He took out his wallet and replaced the three pound notes and drew out a still crackling fiver instead. "This," he said, waving it under Bobby's nose, "is my last offer, my very last offer. Do you understand? It's a great deal of money and you'll be able to buy puppets — spanking new puppets — *and* enough ice-cream and ice-lollies and cakes to make you ill for a fortnight, if that's what you want. How about it?"

Bobby looked at him and at the money for a very long time. He gripped his puppet tightly and then shook his head and pressed his lips tightly together to indicate that he had nothing more to say.

Fred saw the quick look of irritation that passed across the stranger's face and, appalled at the thought of Bobby passing up such an offer, he grasped the child's shoulders and spun him round. "You are a stupid kid," he said. "That's five pounds the man's holding in his hand. Five pounds! Don't be so daft. You take it and give him that horrible doll. Go on!" Bobby looked frightened. Fred had never spoken to him like that before.

"Cut it out!" said Leo sharply. "You're scaring him to death, poor kid. It's his puppet, not yours. You let him make up his own mind. Listen to me, Bobby. Do you want to sell it?" Bobby gazed at him with big eyes and then shook his head so violently that his hair tumbled about. Leo turned to the man. "There you are then. Sorry, but we can't make him if he doesn't want to," and he took hold of Bobby's hand and started to walk away.

The man stood there hesitantly for a moment and then he said, "I do hope your little friend won't regret it later."

Leo halted and then, struck by a sudden thought, turned back to him. "If he does change his mind, where can we get in touch with you?"

The man rubbed his chin thoughtfully. "It might be a little difficult, actually. You see, I'm between houses at the moment, if you know what I mean." Fred shook his head uncomprehendingly. The man took no notice of him. "You'll almost certainly see me about," he went on to Leo. "I'm always round here looking for the odd thing for the collection, you know." He gave them both a cheery wave and strode off.

"How can he be between houses?" asked Fred. "You're either in one or you're not."

"He means he's in the middle of moving," said Leo.

"You must be off your rocker, Leo," Fred said as they set off home at last. "Fancy letting five nicker go down the drain like that. If we'd have taken the puppet off Bobby he'd have howled the place down but he'd have got over it in the end. You know same as I do how much Maggie's mum could have done with the money."

Leo gave Fred a push. "You're the one who's off his rocker," he said. "I told you same as I told the others about that bloke my dad knew who sold the desk that turned out to be worth lots more, didn't I?"

Fred scratched his head thoughtfully. "What's that got to do with it?" he asked. For the life of him he couldn't see what a desk had to do with a puppet.

Leo clapped his hand to his head in despair. "You're as thick as a post, stupid. If the desk was worth a lot why shouldn't Bobby's puppet be worth a lot?"

Fred looked down at the grimy doll. "What? That thing!" he exclaimed incredulously.

"Why not?" said Leo slowly. "He said himself he was a collector, didn't he?"

Fred went on scratching his head. "I don't see what that's got to do with it," he said. "I'm a collector too. I've got all those pictures of wrestlers but I swap them instead of spending thousands of pounds on them." He became confidential. "I'm going to be one. I'm going to call myself . . ."

Leo wasn't interested in his revelations. "It's not the same, you collecting things. Real collectors do pay hundreds and thousands of pounds for things they really want. Alan said so. I bet this chap thought he was onto a good thing because Bobby's only a kid, but if we can find somebody else who collects dolls we might be offered more — or better still, we might manage to find out what it's really worth."

"We don't know anybody else who collects dolls," Fred pointed out. "If we asked any of the barrow-boys they'd give us a clip round the ear."

"Mm," said Leo. "It won't be easy." Then he brightened up. "What about Bernie? He wouldn't think we'd gone round the bend, and even if he doesn't know anything himself he's sure to know somebody who would."

Fred beamed and gave Leo a hefty pat on the back that sent him stumbling into the road. "That's it, Leo! Let's go there now."

"Don't be so daft," said Leo. "You know he's only open on Saturdays. We'll have to wait till then." He shook Bobby to make him pay attention. "Bobby, don't you let anyone touch your puppet. Do you understand? And don't take it to school in case you lose it. If I see you carrying it around I'll get so mad I'll . . . I'll give it to the man who bought you an ice-lolly." He gave Bobby one more shake for luck. "That puppet's got to stay in the house until I tell you you can take it out."

Bobby said absolutely nothing but he grasped the puppet very tightly indeed and nodded solemnly at Leo. Leo was satisfied by this response. The last thing Bobby would want to risk was the loss of it.

By the time they reached Maggie's she and Alan had been there for some time. "Golly!" Maggie exclaimed. "What on earth have you two been up to? I was beginning to be afraid that mum would get here before Bobby and that really would have made her mad."

"Just as we were leaving school Miss Fisher came up and wanted to run through the first scene with Maggie so I stayed on and marked her copy of the play," said Alan.

Fred shook his head reprovingly. "You shouldn't have done that," he said. "Miss Fisher might get mad with you."

"But she asked me to," said Alan patiently.

"I'd get a clump if I marked a book," began Fred. "Why last term Mr Marsh sent me to the head for just filling in all the . . ."

"This is different, Fred." Fred still looked doubtful but Alan couldn't be bothered to explain any further. "And ever since we got here we've been going over her lines. Maggie's learnt a tremendous amount already. I didn't know you'd got such a good memory, Maggie."

Maggie waltzed round Fred with her hands behind her back, her long dark hair swirling about like a cloud. "Have you come to save me?" she asked. "I've been looking for a fisherman's son for days and days."

"Save you?" Fred turned a puzzled gaze on her. "What are you on about? There aren't any fishermen round here. There aren't any fish either."

"She needs one to save her from the dragon," explained Alan. "Only a fisherman's son will do."

Fred's eyes opened wider and he looked at Alan with astonishment. Then a dawning light of comprehension crossed his face. "You're having me on," he said and gave Alan a friendly thump. "Fancy trying to have me on like that. Crikey! You must think I'm thick!"

Bobby thought this was the funniest thing he'd ever heard. He let out a tremendous peal of laughter and reeled about from one person to another. They were still standing in the hall with the front door open and Bobby fell out of the front door and giggled his way down all the steps and then lurched up against a lampost. Then he slid slowly down to the ground, still screaming with laughter and clutching his aching stomach.

Maggie ran down the steps and picked him up and shook him. "Now be quiet, Bobby," she said sternly. "That's enough. You're getting yourself all worked up and if you don't control yourself you'll be crying before long." She glared up at Fred. "That was all your fault," she said as she pushed Bobby inside. "Go in and sit down quietly. I'll be in in a minute."

They all stood together for a few seconds and then suddenly Alan said, "Whatever happened to Marie? I thought she'd change her mind and go with you two."

"Go with us? Not in the kind of mood she was in," said Leo. "She swept past us as if we were something the cat had brought in. She was being all high and mighty. Something must have upset her, but if I'd asked what it was she would only have bitten my head off," and they all nodded together.

Actually Marie was investigating East Westbourne Mews at that moment. After they had all left her, or, as she preferred to put it, let her down, she had decided to do what had been simmering in the back of her mind all day. She had resolved to find out all on her own exactly what Mr Harbottle was up to. There was no doubt at all in her mind that he was a crook, or why else, she thought, would he have been skulking around Maggie's house? Marie was determined not only to get to the bottom of it all but to enjoy the adulation of her friends once again. She could almost hear cries of astonishment ringing in her ears as she visualised herself turning in a real crook to the police. She hurried on to the entrance of the mews determined that whatever happened she wasn't going to leave it again until she'd found out about Mr Harbottle.

East Westbourne Mews was an odd place. It was partly residential and partly used for business. It was also near-derelict. There was a dark and gloomy garage repair shop on one side of it and a small builder's premises on the other. Next to the garage was a little cobbler's shop with a sad collection of shoes in the window and some dessicated strips of leather dangling from the ceiling. She turned away from the shop and looked at the cottages that stretched on either side of the cobbled yard down to the end of the mews. Most of them were empty and crumbling with broken windows and yawning holes where front doors had once been. There were a few of them, however, that were still clearly occupied. These had been brightly painted and there were gay curtains up and a window-box here and there. But in spite of these efforts the mews still looked as if it was quietly dying.

Marie stood there hesitantly. She poked her nose in the dim garage. There was the noise of the hammering of metal, of car engines being raced and of men whistling and laughing in the depths of it. Their voices echoed strangely in the garage. From the cobbler's shop came the gentle but insistent tap tap tap of the cobbler's hammer. But in spite of this, the mews seemed strangely silent and Marie suddenly realised, strangely deserted. There was none of the busy activity of a normal street and it made her feel faintly uneasy.

However, she was not the sort of person to turn back. She went back to the entrance and looked sharply up and down the street to make sure that Harbottle was not approaching and then she walked boldly down the mews as if she had every right to be there. She strolled down the centre of it giving each cottage a brief inspection. She mentally eliminated those that looked particularly well-cared for, since she thought that women probably lived in those and she couldn't believe that Harbottle was married. "You'd have to be desperate," she muttered to herself. When she came to the derelict houses she moved past them rather more quickly, and then returned to the newer ones. Suddenly, sounding like a thunder-clap in the silence of the mews, there was the sharp slam of a door and the sound of heavy footsteps thundering down the stairs of the cottage nearest her. She caught a glimpse of a cap at a window and she looked anxiously up and down the mews. It must be him, she thought. She mustn't be caught spying on him. She darted into the cobbler's shop and tried to hide herself behind the grimy glass door.

There was a little cough from behind. "What can I do for you, young lady," said a tired voice.

Marie didn't bother to turn round. She was too busy trying to catch a glimpse of her quarry. She said the first thing that came into her head. "I'm looking for Mr Harbottle. Do you know where he lives?"

There was another little cough. "No, there's no one of that name round here. I think you've made a mistake."

A large man with a bristly red beard swung past the window. "I think I have," muttered Marie, turning round.

The cobbler was sitting on a high stool at the counter and gazing at her in a mildly curious way through his steel-rimmed spectacles, his thin grey hair falling over his forehead. "I reckon I know every one round here," he said. "Mark you, I should. I've lived here for getting on for thirty years and I shouldn't forget a name . . . "

"Are you sure?" said Marie. "I know he lives here. He's an ordinary sort of man, about forty, and he's got a grey cap and gingery hair, at least, it's not exactly ginger, more sandy than ginger, and light brown eyes and a dark skin and . . . "

The cobbler rubbed his hands on his leather apron "Now I know who you mean," he said, pleased at having identified the man. "You've got the name wrong, young lady, that's what you've done, you've got the name wrong."

"But I haven't," protested Marie. "I know I haven't."

The cobbler shook his head at her. "You young ones are all the same," he said sadly. "You always know best." He picked up his hammer and examined a shoe.

"Oh, sorry," said Marie. She didn't want to upset him. He seemed her only lead now. "I was pretty certain that I . . ."

The cobbler put down his hammer again. "Ah, well," he said magnanimously, "we all make mistakes, don't we?"

Marie twitched impatiently. Why didn't he get on with what he had to say? She managed to keep smiling and nodded in agreement with him. "You were saying . . ."

He smiled triumphantly at her. "Now what you've done is describe a very good friend of mine," he said.

"A good friend of yours?" Marie looked puzzled. What could this mild old man have in common with Harbottle?

"What you've done," the cobbler paused tantalisingly for a moment, "is to describe Tom Smith," he ended.

"Tom Smith!" Marie was dumbfounded.

"Yes, Tom Smith," said the cobbler. "Mind you, it's stretching a point to call him a friend, but he has been living under my roof for the best part of two months now."

"Under your roof?"

The cobbler pointed up to the ceiling with his hammer. "That's right," he said. "Up there. It's funny, you know, he's turned out quite a quiet man to have around." He leaned across the counter confidentially. "To tell the truth, I didn't like the look of him at first. It just shows how wrong you can be. He's out a lot, of course. As a matter of fact you've only just missed him. Do you want to leave a message?"

"Not really," said Marie, trying to sound casual. "I just thought I'd pop in and give him a surprise. I don't suppose you happen to know where he went?"

The cobbler looked up from the shoe he had just taken up again. "Look at this! Just look at this! They must think I'm a magician bringing shoes in like this," and he gave the offending shoe a bang with his hammer to emphasise the point. "Now what was it you said?"

Marie sighed. "I asked if you know where he went."

The cobbler shook his head and banged the shoe about again. "Disgusting!" he said. "Miracles, that's what they expect, miracles." He began jerking nails out of the shoe. "Now let me think," he said. "What was it he said? I've got an idea he said something about going back to do a bit of extra work. Something about meeting his boss in Merton Road. No, that's not right. Perhaps it was Marsden Road."

Marie thought hard. She didn't know of any Marsden Road or Merton Road for that matter. "Could it have been Minster Road?" she asked.

The cobbler put down his tool and took off his glasses and gave them a polish. "I'm not really sure. It could have been. It sounded something like that now I come to think of it."

"What sort of job does he do now?" asked Marie.

The cobbler didn't seem at all suspicious at her questions. He simply seemed delighted to have someone to talk to. "He's never really said, not in so many words, but I think he works in some sort of a factory. Models, that's what they do, model gowns or model railways, that sort of thing. To tell you the truth, I'm not really a curious man. I don't believe in prying into other people's lives. Live and let live that's . . ."

"Thanks very much," said Marie, realising that she wasn't going to get any more out of him. "You've been ever so kind." She opened the door and gave him a bright smile.

"Who shall I say called?" he shouted after her.

"Just say Mata Hari," Marie shouted back.

CHAPTER SIX

When Marie left the mews she felt very elated. In a few minutes she had learned a tremendous amount about Harbottle. He was a newcomer to the neighbourhood just as she'd always thought he was and he was going under an assumed name. Let Alan try and laugh that one off, she thought. She'd been right all along. There was something fishy about him. There was no doubt in her mind as to her next move. She was going straight to Minster Road to see if she could pick up the trail from there.

An hour later, though, she was in a thoroughly bad temper. She had spent most of the time walking up and down the long depressing road in the hopes of at least catching a glimpse of Harbottle or something like a clothing factory. But all there seemed to be were decaying houses left to rot while the whole area waited for redevelopment. She had found the mews strange enough, but this road really gave her the creeps. There was utter silence and a complete lack of movement. Not even a lonely cat stalked up or down it.

"Stupid old fool," she said to herself. "He must have been potty sending me here. There's nothing here except these crummy stinking houses and they're all falling down. He doesn't know what he's talking about. Probably doesn't even know the time of day let alone his own name." She kicked an old tin can into the gutter by way of showing her feelings and then she picked up a stick from the pavement and idly ran it along the railings so that it made a hideous noise.

Joe came round the corner and grinned as he recognised her, a small figure in a long deserted road. He coasted down the slope and came to rest just behind her. He whipped out a pair of spectacles and perched them on the end of his nose. "Aha!" he croaked, "another lover of folk-music, I perceive. Would you care to join our little home-spun circle, a circle searching for truth and simplicity in this horrible materialistic world?"

Marie dropped the stick. "No, I wouldn't Joe," she said. She swung round, a triumphant smile on her face. "See, you didn't fool me this time."

"And how did you know it was me, Miss Sherlock?"

"Because I saw your reflection in that window."

Joe clapped his hand to his head and staggered back as if stunned. "What a sleuth! You ought to be in my department. Who would have thought there could be any reflections in those grubby panes. Ah, well, back to business. Are you going to join the music cirle?"

Marie looked at him warily. "There isn't any circle," she said, "is there?"

"No," admitted Joe. He tried the glasses on Marie and shook his head. "No, they're not you. But we could have a circle. Hundreds, nay thousands, would join. We could call it the Marie Jenkins Homespun Circle. What about it, Cecilia?" He grabbed the lampost and skipped round it. "We could bring back maypoles, bring back . . ."

"Fancy carrying on like that. You are awful," said Marie in a disapproving voice, although really she was always entertained by Joe. "Anyone would think you were bonkers. Don't you care what people think of you?"

Joe stopped skipping and drew closer to her. "The people," he whispered, "are nothing but a flock of particularly stupid sheep. The day is dawning though, my sunflower, when we shall send them all back down the mines while we, the brave, the beautiful . . ."

"The barmy," said Marie.

"Barmy!" cried Joe. "What a thing to say!"

"Well, you must be," said Marie, "or you wouldn't waste your time the way you do. Most of the time I bet you don't know what you're talking about yourself."

Joe dragged out a handkerchief and dabbed at his eyes. "Found out!" he cried brokenly. "My little secret discovered. And to think I thought you were a mere ignoramus, an illiterate poppet."

"Come off it, Joe," Marie said, feeling embarrassed. She knew he wasn't really crying, but she felt uncomfortable standing by his side while his shoulders heaved and he wiped his eyes.

Jo whipped the handkerchief away and stuck his thumbs in his belt. "O.K. then, baby. What are you doing in this nauseous neighbourhood?"

Marie eyed him uncertainly. "Promise you won't laugh."

Joe licked his finger and drew it silently across his throat. "Promise," he said.

Satisfied with this display Marie began to tell him all about her recent encounter with the cobbler and how Harbottle was living with him under the name of Smith.

"I'd probably change my name too if I'd been saddled with Harbottle," said Joe. "One can't really call it a pretty name now can one?"

"If only I could find the factory where he's supposed to

work," said Marie, "I might be able to get to the bottom of it all on my own, but I'm not even sure this is the right road."

Joe took hold of her chin and tipped it up so that she was forced to look him straight in the eye. "Whatever you do, Marie," he said in a serious tone, "don't hang round here. It's not a pleasant place and, as you can see, it's remarkably deserted. You hop along home and I'll pop in and see you later and we'll think of the best way of dealing with the horrible Harbottle together."

"So you think he sounds fishy, too?"

"Unsavoury, shall we say? I must have a word with some rather nice uniformed gentlemen I know. Perhaps they've heard a whisper about him," said Joe thoughtfully. "Now be good, Marie, and push off."

Marie looked at him pleadingly. "Can't you come back with me now, Joe? I haven't anyone at all now. They all went off with Maggie and left me alone," she added pathetically.

"And I've no doubt it was all your own selfish little fault. And it's no good looking at me with those big blue eyes, my dear little mangel-worzel. I can't come with you now but I really will see you later."

"Why not?" asked Marie petulantly.

Joe pointed up at the sky. "The sun sets! Duty calls! Even for you, O Queen of the Cabbage Patch, I cannot let my public down." He got on his scooter and started the engine and then he looked again at Marie. "Now remember, apple blossom, horrible Harbottle is a nasty man. Go home and write it out ten thousand times."

Sullenly Marie watched him accelerate up the road and disappear from view. "He's just a stinker like everyone else," she muttered. "Self, self, self, that's all he thinks about." Then she turned and made for home. Although the street was not in her territory she had been up and down it so many times that evening that she felt almost at home in it. Idly she sauntered down the derelict street, staring at the broken windows and the bits of corrugated iron that were stuck over some of them, at the foul overflowing dustbins and the peeling paint. "I'd rather be dead than live in a dump like this," she thought. "Same thing, really."

She passed the high brick wall with a pair of iron gates that formed one corner of a side road. She had passed the wall often before, but, struck by a sudden thought, she continued round the corner and followed the spiked wall until that too ended in a pair of tall iron gates. She crossed the road and looked at the building beyond the wall. Yes, there was no doubt about it. It concealed a building of some sort, probably a factory. She stared at the wall topped with spikes and bits of broken glass. It must be to stop the workers escaping, she thought. Nobody in their right minds could possibly want to get in. Even standing on tiptoe she could only see part of the first floor of the building, and she felt a secret sort of relief at there being no sign of life in it. She could simply go back and tell Joe about it.

Just as she was shrugging her shoulders and turning away a flicker of movement caught her eye. She stared up. There was nothing. Puzzled, she moved across to the far side of the road. From there she could see the upper part of the factory more clearly. As she stood there a figure appeared momentarily at the window — a figure carrying a cap and a raincoat. Heart in mouth, fearful of being spotted, Marie ducked and ran doubled up to the shelter of the wall. It was Harbottle. It had to be Harbottle. She'd tracked him down at last.

Her eyes glittered with excitement as she pressed herself against the wall. Now she had to decide what to do next. If she went home and waited for Joe to come she stood a good chance of losing Harbottle again, so that didn't seem like a very good idea. The only other thing to do was to wait for Harbottle to come out and trail him herself. She knew the time was getting on but he couldn't, she reasoned, be very long, not if he'd got his cap and raincoat ready to put on. It was a good thing, she thought, that there was a padlock on the factory gates. If there hadn't been she might have had to consider going in after him and she didn't fancy that idea very much. No, she'd do much better to wait for him. Anyway she wasn't keen on sharing the glory with Joe when she'd done all the work herself. Yes, she'd wait — but where?

She looked around. Almost opposite the factory was a near-derelict chapel, its yellow stucco walls peeling in a disgusting way as though it suffered from an unpleasant disease. There were seven steps leading up to it and on the top of them was a large easel with a faded red poster saying "Repent" in big black letters. Beneath it a smaller one simply said "Bingo. Saturday". It seemed an ideal place to Marie. She ran quietly up the steps and squatted down behind the easel and tried to make herself comfortable. A much older notice on the reverse side of the easel stared down at her. "He seest Thou" it said. Marie glanced at it. "Crikey! I hope not," she said with a nervous giggle.

It wasn't long before she felt hopelessly cramped. Every time she tried to stretch the easel rocked dangerously backwards and forwards, so she concentrated on wriggling her toes instead. She hummed to herself for a bit and rehearsed her new dramatic story. She was almost reduced to saying multiplication tables to relieve the boredom when suddenly she tensed. There were sounds coming from the factory. A door was slammed, there was the clump of heavy boots and then a cheerful whistling. Someone from behind the gates fiddled with the lock and they swung open.

Wide-eyed, Marie peered from behind the easel.

"Blast!" she said furiously. It wasn't Harbottle at all. It was a small man in overalls. Still whistling, the man bent over the padlock, straightened up and then walked briskly down the road.

"He's still there then," said Marie to herself. She wriggled from behind her shelter and looked at the locked gates for a moment. Then she went round to the Minster Road gates. They were closed, but looking at them Marie suddenly realised that she could have missed Harbottle. While she was watching one side there was nothing to have stopped him from going out of the other. Furious with herself, she gave the gates a violent kick. Slowly, silently, smoothly, invitingly, they swung open.

Hesitantly, Marie moved forward and put one foot inside the grounds. Almost reluctantly she took another step. She looked round anxiously. There was no sound, no movement. She slipped in and sheltered behind one of the gates. Her heart seemed to be thumping abnormally loudly as she stood there. What was she to do next? Two steps and she would reach safety again, but somehow Marie couldn't bring herself to take them. She had to know if Harbottle was still there.

Taking a deep breath she moved towards the main door of the building. Quietly she turned the handle and pushed. It opened easily and she sidled silently through it and closed it behind her. To her consternation she found that she was now in almost total darkness. The only glimmer of light came from two dirty panes of glass set high in the top of the door.

After a second or two Marie's eyes became accustomed to the dark and she could dimly make out a passage ending in a pair of double doors with a door about half-way down on either side. Keeping her back to the wall, she slipped down the corridor. Suddenly, from the door in the right, came the sharp sound of a cough. Marie froze. She stood rigid, hardly daring to breathe, fearful that Harbottle would emerge and she'd be caught. Something jabbed her in the back and she put one hand behind her and felt a door knob. Carefully, slowly, she twisted it, edged the door open and slithered into the safety of the room. Just as quietly she closed it and leaned against it, her fingers in her mouth.

There was another cough and the sound of heavy footsteps from the room opposite. There were strange sounds: something was being dragged about and there was heavy breathing. Marie completely covered her mouth. Suppose her breathing sounded as loud as that! She tried to breathe steadily and evenly for a few minutes and then she suddenly realised that there was silence again. She waited a few minutes, listening intently at the door, but there was nothing. Carefully she opened the door just a crack and waited again. Still nothing. She opened it a little wider and risked poking her head round for an instant to flash a glance up and down the passage. It was empty, totally empty and utterly still, and it was also much darker. She began to feel afraid. One more try, she promised herself, just one more attempt to get a glimpse of Harbottle and then she'd leave this hateful, menacing building.

Silently she slipped over to the opposite door and put her ear to it. There was a sudden scraping sound and then the flare of a match. Holding her breath, Marie bent down to the keyhole, but her movement made the door creak. The tension was too much. Her nerve broke. She fled to the doors at the end of the corridor, her arms stretched out in front of her. As her fingertips touched them they swung inwards. At the same time she heard the rattle of Harbottle's door knob. She looked around, panic-stricken. She couldn't hope to reach her old sanctuary. Neither could she possibly reach the front door. The click of a light switch decided her. She slipped through the double doors and found herself in total darkness. In the distance she heard a door bang and then there was the sudden petrifying sound of footsteps clumping towards her. Fearfully she moved away from the door, her arms in front of her, quite unable to see anything at all. The footsteps stopped outside the door. They halted and then they receded again.

Marie, tense and frightened, stood stock still, straining her ears for any sound at all. There was nothing. He was gone. She let out her breath: a long, low sigh of relief. Carefully she felt her way back to the door. Her confident hands felt nothing. There was only space. She opened her eyes wider, as if she could push back the curtain of darkness. The door must be there! It had to be there! In panic she swung round and round, making futile grasping movements. It was as if she was fumbling inside a cloud: there was nothing to get hold of, nothing to grasp. Mindless now of any noise she might make, she stumbled around the room, more afraid of the dark than of Harbottle. The room seemed curiously empty and she moved blindly from one place to another, all sense of direction lost. Suddenly she tripped herself up and fell heavily against a wall. She clung gratefully to it for a moment, finding comfort in its very solidity. Gradually the feeling of panic departed and common sense asserted itself. Doors were to be found in walls. As long as she didn't lose the wall she would find the door. Marie moved carefully along it, one hand brushing its smooth surface and then, with an upsurge of confidence, she felt the edge of a door.

With a little cry of thankfulness Marie pushed it open — and then she cried aloud in despair. The other side of the door offered nothing other than more darkness. Where was the light that should have come from the windows at the end of the corridor? She strained her eyes. There wasn't even the slightest glimmer. Steady, she said to herself. Don't be silly. It's dark outside, that's why it's dark inside. She had only to go straight down the corridor and then she'd reach the outside and safety. Holding her arms straight out in front of her once more, she stepped forward — and then she screamed. She screamed and screamed again as her hands touched smooth, soft hair and a cold, cold face. And she dropped to the floor.

Meanwhile Maggie and the boys were still together when there was a thunderous knock on the door. "I'll go," said Maggie. "I bet it's Marie." She flung it open. Joe stood there.

"Where's Marie?" he said urgently.

"Marie?"

"Yes. Do you know where she is?"

"No. I haven't seen her since we left school."

"Alan here?" Maggie nodded. Joe brushed past her and walked into the kitchen. "Have you seen Marie?"

Alan put his cup down. "What's up?" he asked. He'd never seen Joe worried before.

"You haven't seen her then?"

The boys shook their heads. "What's wrong?" asked Leo.

"She hasn't been home yet," said Joe tersely.

Maggie glanced up at the clock. "But it's gone eight," she said incredulously.

"You're positive you haven't seen her?" They all shook their heads. "Then I was the last to see her," said Joe, "and that was nearly two hours ago in Minster Road. Do all your parents know where you are?" They nodded. "Then that's all right. Alan, you come with me on my scooter. Leo, you and Fred follow as fast as you can. You'd better stay here Maggie, because you can't leave Bobby anyway. If Marie should turn up before your mother gets back, leave Marie with him and come and tell us she's safe." Joe rushed out again, Alan on his heels.

The moment they reached Minster Road Joe stopped the scooter. "Get off here, Alan, and work your way down the street. Look everywhere: in every doorway and side passage, behind the hoardings, down in the basements, and look through the windows of those derelict houses if you can. Go into them if you can't see."

"What shall I do if I can't get in?" asked Alan.

"Break a window," said Joe grimly. "This road has got to be searched properly. I'll begin working my way down from the other end of the road. When the others arrive, keep Leo and send Fred up to me."

As he roared off again Alan began a thorough search. He overlooked nothing and even made his way into overgrown back gardens and pushed open the doors of rotting sheds and outhouses. It wasn't long before the others arrived and they went on searching, saying little to each other. Slowly the two groups grew closer and closer together until Alan realised, a sinking feeling in his stomach, that there was nowhere else to look. They all went through the last house together.

Joe shook his head as they came out. "It's no good," he said seriously. "I shall have to go to her mother and advise her to go down to the station."

"Station?" said Fred. "Do you think she's gone on a train or something?"

"Police station," explained Leo.

"Mrs Jenkins wasn't really worried when I saw her earlier because she thought Marie was with Maggie. But the situation now seems rather serious to me. We haven't any choice. The police are the only people who are competent to deal with this sort of thing."

The boys looked in a depressed way at each other.

107

"Perhaps she went off to see someone," suggested Leo.

"She'd got some crackpot idea of tracking down that bloke she think's a crook," said Alan thoughtfully. "She's got a real bee in her bonnet about him."

"I know all about that," said Joe grimly. "She'd already tracked him as far as here. It's all my fault in a way. I should have seen her home, but I was certain I'd persuaded her to leave. He's not the sort of person any girl should tangle with."

"What do you know about him?" asked Alan anxiously.

"Practically nothing," admitted Joe. "I only caught a glimpse of him myself, but when I described him to — to some friends of mine, they seemed very interested."

"Do you mean the cops?" asked Fred suddenly.

"Yes," said Joe. "I've got a couple of friends in the force. I'm not sure yet whether he's got a record or not, but they'll find out. Whether he has or whether he hasn't is unimportant now. What is important is the fact that Marie really seems to have disappeared and it seems to me that it's a job for the police."

"But if you go and tell her mum and she's really all right she'll get into a terrible row," argued Leo. "Can't we think of somewhere else to look first?"

Joe looked troubled. "The longer we wait," he said gravely, "the harder it'll be to trace her. This must be reported I'm afraid."

There seemed nothing more they could say and they turned miserably away. As they did so, a small man in overalls came out of a side road and round the corner. He was passing a pair of iron gates set in the wall when something caught his eye and he went back. Whistling tunelessly to himself he bent down and fumbled with the lock. "Dratted thing," he said aloud. "I could have sworn I locked it." He fumbled in his pockets and pulled out a bunch of keys, selected one and turned it in the padlock. He gave the gates a hard push to make sure they would stay shut and then strolled away, still whistling.

Leo rushed after him. "Hey!" he shouted. "Stop!"

The man swung round in alarm, but seeing only a scruffy boy hurtling along towards him he waited. "Well, what do you want?" he asked.

"When does that factory close?"

"Six, only I don't get away till seven."

"You didn't see a girl with long fair hair round here about then, did you?" asked Leo. Then with a sudden flash of brilliance, he added "Or even trying to get in?"

The man shook his head. "No one could have got in after I left. I lock up, and I had a good look round first, like I always do. What's this all about?"

"We've lost our friend," said Leo, trying to sound casual. "I suppose when you go the factory's empty?"

"Well, Mr Parks was there, but I know he was going to leave just after me because I got his cap and mac for him." He was beginning to look curious. "Why should she want to get in here?"

"I don't suppose she did," said Leo. "It was just that we couldn't think of anything else. We just wondered if she could have been shut in by accident."

"Impossible!" The man was emphatic. "I locked these gates myself and Mr Parks was going to lock the others, and being the manager he's very particular about it. Sorry I can't help you." He turned away and walked briskly down the road.

Leo returned dejectedly to the others. "No good," he said "He said no one was around when he left and no one could have got in afterwards because he locked the gates himself."

They all looked at each other, their faces anxious and strained. Joe glanced at his watch. "Well that settles it . . ."

"Joe!" It was Leo again, tugging at his sleeve impatiently. "He said he'd locked the gates himself, but he's just done it all over again, so either he didn't do it properly in the first place or he didn't do it at all. So Marie could have got in, couldn't she?"

"She's nosey enough," observed Fred.

"She's stubborn enough," said Joe. "Do you know, I think there's just a chance Leo might be right. It is the only factory round here and she was nattering on about one. Look, we mustn't waste too much time. We'll just have a quick look around. Come on, we'll try the gates in the side road." He gave them a push. "Bother! They really are locked. Well, there's nothing else for it. We'll just have to go over the wall."

"What for?" asked Fred.

"To get in," said Alan shortly.

"Why don't we just go through the other ones?"

"Don't be so dim," snapped Alan. "You might as well say why don't we fly to the moon."

Joe looked thoughtfully at the wall. He gazed at the spikes and the broken glass. "This is going to be a bit tricky," he said, taking off his sweater. "Alan, you know the alley we passed? There are some old orange boxes in it. Go and get the strongest one you can find."

Alan was back in a couple of minutes with quite a large one. "I'm going to stand on it," Joe explained. "I only hope it's as strong as it looks. Leo, I'm going to hoist you up on my shoulders and then straighten up. You should just be able to reach the spikes — use my sweater to protect your hands — and then you'll be able to heave yourself up. I'll help Fred up after you and Alan will go last. You've got the tricky bit to do, Alan. Somehow you've got to balance yourself up there and manage to give me a hand up. Fred, while I'm giving Leo a bunk up I want . . ." Joe stopped and looked around. "Where's Fred?"

They all turned round. Fred had vanished. "We can't wait for him," said Joe. He bent down. "Up you get on my shoulders, Leo." Helped by Alan, Leo scrambled up and Joe stepped onto the box. Leo swayed a bit as Joe straightened up. He stretched out and almost grasped the spikes.

"Lean forward a bit, Joe," he said, and as Joe did so he managed to grip them. "O.K." Joe grunted and seized Leo's ankles and heaved him up. Leo scrabbled around and got onto the wall. "Just missed the glass," he said. He looked down into the yard. "Shall I jump? It's not far. There's a kind of bank underneath."

"No, hang on for a bit and keep a sharp eye open. We'll have a difficult time explaining if we get caught. And now I come to think of it, Alan might need your help when it's my turn.

Alan went next, and although it was harder on Joe, it was a bit easier for Alan than it had been for Leo, since he was taller. He reached a spike with comparative ease and clambered up. "Your turn, Joe," he said.

Holding on to the spike with one hand, Alan dangled the other as near to Joe as possible. Joe stood on his toes on the box, his arms stretched high in the air. Alan managed to grasp one wrist and somehow Joe fought his way up the wall. "Pull!" he gasped. Leo bent down and grabbed the other wrist and although they were almost slipping off themselves they succeeded in dragging Joe up high enough for him to release one hand and grip a spike. With great effort he hauled himself up and joined them on the wall. He waited until he'd got his breath back and then he peered down the bank. "It's

111

not a bad drop," he said. "Face the wall, dangle from the spikes and let go."

They all three turned round, slithered down as far as possible, and then dropped. As they picked themselves up they found Fred gazing at them curiously.

"What shall we do next?" he asked.

"How did you get in?" demanded Alan.

"Like I said, through the gates. I could see you only had to jiggle the padlock a bit to get it open."

"But we all saw the man lock it," said Leo.

"I've seen locks like that before," said Fred contemptuously. "Child's play, that's what they are."

"Well at least Fred's made it easy for us to get out," said Joe. He dropped his voice. "Now, keep your voices down. I know the place is supposed to be empty, but you never know. I don't want to be caught. It might be rather embarrassing. We'd better stick together in case we have to make a dash for it. I don't want to have to chase round collecting you up one by one. No one's to stray. Is that understood?"

There were mutters of agreement and Joe stole forward and tried the main door. It was locked. He padded round the side of the building until he came to some ground floor windows. Alan and Leo, following closely behind, hardly made a sound. Fred managed to step on every piece of paper and to kick every stone in his path, in spite of frequent shushings from the others. At last Joe stopped by one of the windows and examined it carefully. He gave a self-satisfied nod and pulled a pen-knife from his pocket. "Lucky I've got my burglar's kit with me," he muttered. He wriggled the knife to and fro between the window frame and the pane and then, with a quick flip, released the catch. He pushed the window open and climbed in. He helped the others to follow him one by one.

"It's dark," moaned Fred. "Can't we have the light on?" There were indignant hissings from all sides and Fred was reduced to silence.

Joe felt his way carefully round the walls until he reached the door. "This way," he whispered. But they stumbled over each other and made such a noise that he said in a low angry voice, "Any more of that and you'll have to wait outside." They froze into silence.

Joe felt for the light switch. "Alan, go back to the window. I felt a blind. Go and let it down. We must have a little light."

"O.K." Alan crept back to the window. There was a sharp click and a rustling sound. "I've done it."

Joe snapped the light on. They were in a perfectly ordinary office. He opened the door and took a quick look down the corridor and, motioning the boys to stay where they were, took a long stride into the room opposite. It was empty. He came back. "There are double doors at the end of this passage," he said quietly. "We'll take a look in there next. Now we'll have to be quick if we don't want the light to be seen outside." He stepped into the corridor once more and stood by the light switch near the main door. "Down to the room at the end of the passage as quickly and quietly as possible," he ordered. "Last one out switch that light off and shut the door."

Alan saw the others out, switched the light off and shut the door. Joe switched his light on. Nothing happened. "Damn!" he said. "Switch yours on again, Alan, and leave the door open a bit. It'll give us a bit of light."

Leo, who was in front, led the way to the double doors, followed by the others. Alan hurried after them. The closer they got to the doors the more shadowy and gloomy it became. The light behind them was only a feeble glimmer. Leo pushed open the doors and tiptoed in. He had just made out the outlines of more double doors on the far side of the room, when Fred, who was holding the doors open as the others went through, suddenly let them swing back and the faint light was completely cut off.

Anxiously Fred blundered about in the rear while Joe and Leo, with Alan close behind them, pushed on into the next room. Leo tripped and crashed heavily to the floor, letting go of the door at the same time. The door swung back and hit Joe squarely in the face. With a loud cry he reeled back, knocking Alan over and then landing on top of him. Leo, scrabbling around on the floor, felt something brushing against his face. "It's hair!" he yelled. "It's hair!"

Fred blundered across the outer room at hearing these cries of distress and charged the door shoulder first. Alan, struggling to his feet, was thrown to the floor again, but this time he grabbed grimly at the legs of his unseen enemy and brought him down as well. Together they rolled through the door fighting and kicking each other furiously. Alan drew back his fist and clouted Fred straight in the eye. Fred let out a bellow of pain but grabbed at another pair of legs. Joe crashed on top of him.

"I've got him!" shouted Fred.

"It's me, you fool, it's me!" yelled Joe. He felt around for something to get a grip on and grabbed Leo's pullover. Leo totally panic-stricken, kicked hard to free himself and hacked Alan on the shins. Breathing hard, Alan thumped him back "Help!" cried Leo. "They're over here!"

Fred, now being pummelled by Joe, who was desperately trying to free himself, managed to squirm across the room and seize a leg. He grabbed hold of it and pulled as hard as he could. He bellowed loudly as he felt its smooth surface. "It's got nothing on!" and tugged furiously at it again.

"Here!" shouted Leo, now astride Alan.

Alan twisted his ear. "Help!" he bawled. "I've got him!"

"I'll fix you!" snorted Joe, banging Fred's head on the ground.

"Take that," snarled Leo, as he punched Alan in the stomach, "and that!"

Fred, dazed by the pounding Joe was giving him, gripped the leg he was still holding and gave it a sudden jerk. "The leg's come away in my hand!" he roared. "I've pulled off his leg!"

There was a moment of silence. Joe's hand touched the wall. He groped along it, feeling for a light switch. The uproar broke out again: grunting, shouting, thumping and yelling. Thankfully he felt the switch at last. He snapped it on.

The sudden light dazzled them all and they lay about in a state of utter confusion. Fred lay stretched out, his eyes closed and his mouth open. Alan was sprawled across him, his hands entangled in Fred's hair. Leo had Alan's feet in one hand and a tattered wig in the other. In the corner, half-hidden by the door, dirty and tear-stained and dishevelled, was Marie. She was brandishing a piece of wood, clearly determined to defend herself if she had to. Joe, by now completely exhausted, grasped the edge of the door and laughed helplessly, while Marie burst into floods of tears and the boys looked at each other in a shamefaced manner as the silent row of waxen models simpered down at them.

CHAPTER SEVEN

"And what did Joe say after that?" asked Maggie eagerly. I
was the following Monday, and the first time she had been
allowed to see Marie since they had left the factory and she
was anxious to hear all about it.

Marie buried her head in the cushions of the settee. "He
just said 'So long, Mata Hari,' " she muttered indistinctly
And then she suddenly sat up again. "That's what he keep
calling me," she added crossly, "and I haven't seen him since
and I don't care if I never do again."

"How long have you got to stay here?" asked Maggie
sympathetically, looking round the dazzlingly clean bu
chilly front room.

Marie shrugged. "I don't know. She only let me com
downstairs today. I was in bed the rest of the time. All sh
keeps on saying is that I've had a nasty shock and I know
that anyway. If she really knew what had happened she'
have a nasty shock herself. Perhaps I ought to tell her an
then they'd put her in a bin and then maybe I could go ou
again."

"You are awful," said Maggie reprovingly. "Of course sh
was worried. She wouldn't be much of a mother if she wasn
and then you'd really have something to moan about."

"Oh, stop lecturing me," said Marie peevishly. "Tell me what's been going on in school. I could have gone if she'd have let me. I could even have gone out on Saturday really, but she keeps on and on about delayed shock."

"We didn't do anything on Saturday, so you didn't miss much," said Maggie. "It was pouring all day long. Oh, I'll tell you something. Leo's dad gave him some pocket money."

Marie bounced right up. "Leo's dad! That's a turn up all right. He must have got softening of the brain all of a sudden. It's rotten the way he treats Leo, isn't it?"

"I don't suppose he thinks about it much," said Maggie.

"That's the trouble," said Marie, twisting round and giving a cushion a bash. "He only remembers Leo when he happens to get in his way. Anyway, I don't want to talk about him. I just want to know what went on at school. Did old Marsh give that English test?"

"No," said Maggie. "They had Miss Tolly instead. I wasn't there because I was rehearsing, but I heard all about it. It was another of those mad lessons. This time everyone had to pretend to be in a band, so they all went stark raving mad as usual and started honking and hooting and tinging away and Pat went completely off her rocker and rushed around hitting everyone on the head and screaming 'Ping' every time she did it. You can guess what happened next."

"Mr Marsh!"

"Yes. Trouble, trouble, trouble."

"Just my luck," said Marie gloomily. "Missed all that."

"And you didn't miss the English test."

"I never get out of anything."

"They say she's leaving. I don't know why they keep on having drama students. They're never any good."

"Some of them are," said Marie warmly. "That Mr Thomas was and so was Mr Goodwin. Weren't they good-looking!"

Maggie gave her a nudge. "Trust you to remember the handsome ones."

"Course I do," said Marie unabashed. "It doesn't happen very often. Anyway, go on. What else has happened?"

Marie thought hard. "Oh, I know. Bill Spense got caught letting down old Markham's tyres. You can guess what happened to him!"

"Serve him right," said Marie callously. "Stupid clot. Fancy letting himself get caught."

Mrs Jenkins came clattering down the passage and bustled in. She tugged the rug tightly round Marie and then put her hand on her forehead while Marie wriggled around impatiently. "Don't think I'm not pleased to see you, Maggie," she said, "but I really think you ought to be running along. I don't want Marie getting over-excited."

"Oh, mum," said Marie wearily. "I keep telling you there's nothing wrong with me now. All I needed was a good long sleep and you've kept me shut up for days now. I want to get up."

"I might let you up for half an hour or so this evening," said Mrs Jenkins with the air of one conferring a great favour, "but don't count on it. You don't exactly look yourself yet and I don't want to take any chances. Being shut up in a place like that and banging away and not a soul to hear you might leave a scar for ever."

"A scar!" Marie looked incredulous.

"On your mind, Marie." Mrs Jenkins turned to Maggie. "I want you out of this room in exactly five minutes, Maggie. Marie's had quite enough excitement for one day. Now don't forget, five minutes," she repeated as she went out of the room.

Marie had gone bright red while her mother was speaking. Maggie waited until she heard the bang of the kitchen door and then she turned to Marie and said curiously, "What *did* Joe tell your mother?"

"Don't you laugh!" said Marie fiercely. "I'll never speak to you again if you do. He told her I was shut in a ladies' lavatory for hours and hours, and if I ever find out you've told anyone I'll . . . I'll scratch your eyes out!"

Inwardly Maggie started shaking but she managed to control herself and keep a straight face. "I won't tell," she said earnestly, "I swear I won't. But what on earth made Joe think up a story like that? He is rotten."

"Actually I think it was pretty clever of him. You know I was in a terrible mess and I couldn't possibly have told her the truth. You know what she's like." Maggie nodded understandingly. "You've heard her carrying on about manners and being polite and all that, and especially about being a lady, haven't you? Well, being like that she thinks it isn't nice to talk about things like lavatories to anyone, especially a man, so she couldn't ask Joe for any details and she can't bring herself to mention it to me and she hasn't even called the doctor, because she'd have to explain it to him, so really I've got off pretty lightly."

"Mm. There wouldn't half have been a row if she had known," Maggie agreed. "Really you had more bad luck than anything else. Anyone might have mistaken the manager of the factory for Harbottle. Did you know that Joe went to see him? I don't know what he said but he's fixed it so that the manager isn't even going to complain."

"What about Harbottle?" asked Marie eagerly. "Has anyone seen him?"

Maggie shrugged. "I don't think so. I don't honestly think anyone cares. After all, you don't really know anything, do you. All you've been doing is guessing."

Marie looked stubborn. "All right. You don't have to

119

believe me, but I know I'm right. You'll see I am one day."
She changed the subject. "How's the play going?"

"Smashing!" cried Maggie enthusiastically. "It's even
better with Alan in it and Miss . . ."

"Alan! Is he in it?" Marie was put out. "What's he in it
for? He's the world's lousiest actor."

"Didn't you know he'd got a part?"

Marie thumped her cushion. "How could I know?" she
snapped. "I've been stuck in bed, haven't I? No one's
bothered to come and tell me anything . . ."

"But I've come every day," protested Maggie. "Your
mother wouldn't let me in before."

Marie took no notice of her. She bashed the cushion even
more viciously. "Alan! They must have been desperate. He's
a terrible actor. He's hopeless. He's worse . . ." Her mind
searched for a suitable comparison. "He's worse than Fred!"

"Fred's not all that bad," said Maggie loyally. "I mean he's
not exactly good, but he will be when Miss Fisher's finished
with him. Anyway, as a soldier . . ."

"Fred!" Marie was aghast. "You can't mean he's in it
too!" She stared at Maggie and Maggie nodded slowly.
Marie's temper rose. "It's not fair! It's just not fair. Everybody's in it except me and I'm a better actor than any of
you. You know I am. And what am I supposed to do while
you're all rehearsing? Stand by and clap, I suppose. Well, if
that's what you think, you've got another think coming."
Her voice rose higher and higher. "Let me tell you I'm going
to be far too busy to waste my time on a stupid little play, so
even if you went down on your bended knees and crawled I
still wouldn't come. Leo and I . . ."

Maggie took a deep breath. "Leo's in it too."

Marie went quite white. "Then that's it! If you've got that
thick-witted, half-baked idiot in it then I'm glad I'm not.

You'll be the laughing stock of the Portobello."

By this time Maggie was furious too. It was as much as she could do to sit still instead of smacking Marie's face. "Look here," she said icily, "it's not their fault they got chosen when you weren't there. Why don't you come straight out with it and admit that you're jealous of all of us, because that's what's wrong. You're straight-forward ordinary jealous!"

Marie slumped down and shut her eyes. "Shut up! Just shut up! Shut up and clear off! Don't bother to come back!"

Maggie jumped to her feet and stood over Marie, her eyes flashing and her palm itching. "Don't you worry, I won't. You won't ever be bothered with me again. As far as I'm concerned, that's it." She flung out of the room and slammed the door as loudly as she could and rushed out into the street to where the boys were waiting for her.

"How is she?" asked Leo anxiously.

"Bad-tempered," said Maggie briefly.

"What for?"

"It's the play," said Maggie. "She's so jealous because you're all in . . ."

"She can have my part," said Fred generously. He'd had trouble learning his two lines.

"She can't be a soldier," Leo pointed out. "They're all boys. She can't have my part either. She'd look daft as an old man."

"I wonder if Miss Fisher could find a part for her," murmured Maggie, but she didn't sound too enthusiastic.

"Why should she?" said Alan unexpectedly, and they all stared at him in surprise. He usually took Marie's part. "It won't do her any harm," he went on, looking a bit pink in the face. "What with one thing and another she's been nothing but a pain in the neck recently. It'll do her good not to be first for once. Let her try and get round us for a

121

change instead of us having to get round her, if you see what I mean," he finished lamely.

There was a moment of silence as they digested this revolutionary point of view. "That's right," said Leo. "Anyway, she'll have forgotten what it was all about in a day or two. You know Marie."

Maggie remained silent but Fred grunted an agreement. "Yes," he said. "That's what I think. Come on. We'll be late for Miss Fisher."

They all turned back to school. Miss Fisher had been forced to have rehearsals after school ever since Ann Lucas had triggered off the outbreak of chicken-pox. Most of the original cast had caught it from each other and she had had to find a lot of substitutes. The performance was fixed for the following Saturday and so she had had to make time for a lot of extra rehearsals. Much to her surprise the cast had become amazingly enthusiastic, and turned up whether they were needed or not.

When they arrived they went straight to the school hall and stood looking at the stage, which was empty except for three chairs which represented the castle. Miss Fisher, who was in the corner talking to a couple of boys, looked up and smiled as they entered. "Good," she said briskly. "Dead on time. Now we're going to do scene two. I want Maggie behind the castle wall looking forlorn, and I want the King and Queen in the front of the stage. Now remember, you're quarrelling, you're having a really raging row. Soldiers, you line up in your correct order in the wings. I want you ready to march the moment you hear your cue. We still haven't got the rifles, but pretend they are in your arms. Leo, put your chair in the usual place. As the story-teller you must see that you're always in exactly the same place. Now think! You're very old, so you must sit slumped, as if you hope you'll never

122

have to get up again. No matter what happens you are not to look round. "Where is the fisherman's son? Oh, there you are, Michael. Your entrance is immediately after the soldiers, so you want to be ready right behind them. Are you all right?" She waited a minute. "Right then, Maggie, you're on!"

Instead of the immediate response she had hoped for everyone was looking over her shoulder. She turned round. Fred was in the middle of the hall standing absolutely erect. She clapped her hands to her head, a look of astonishment on her face. "And what exactly do you think you are doing, Fred?"

Fred looked at her. "Lining up," he said, surprised. "You said we'd got to line up."

"Not where you stand for prayers, Fred," she said patiently. "I mean over there, in the wings."

Fred looked round doubtfully as if he expected to see a bird or two fluttering about. "Behind me, nut-case!" hissed one of the soldiers, and with a grateful look Fred ambled over and joined the file.

At a glance from Miss Fisher, Maggie began. She sighed. "I'm tired of being in prison. I'm tired of being neglected. I've been here for weeks and weeks and weeks and no one cares, no one . . ."

Miss Fisher held up her hand. "We don't want such a tragic one, Maggie. I only want you to *look* tragic. Remember, this is really a joke. The whole play is making fun of fairy stories, so try and sound a little lighter."

Maggie continued her speech. Beneath the castle walls the King and the Queen appeared.

"Can't we go home?" said the King plaintively. "I want my tea. Besides, I can't remember what we're looking for."

"Speak for yourself," said the Queen. "Of course, at your

123

age it's not surprising your memory is bad, but mine, why mine is as fresh as . . . as fresh as . . ."

"A stale egg," said the King helpfully. The Queen flounced off

Miss Fisher sat back and relaxed. The rehearsal was going very smoothly, she thought. Most of the cast seemed to know their lines and their moves. Only Fred caused a minor upset when he suddenly realised that the rest of the soldiers were marching away, leaving him behind. Trying to catch up with them, he bumped into Leo's chair and Leo shot straight onto the floor.

"Fred! Be careful," called Miss Fisher once order had been restored. "Keep your eyes on the boy in front." So Fred went through the rest of the rehearsal with his eyes glued to the boy in front of him. It looked a bit odd to see him marching around like that but Miss Fisher felt it was better than having him blunder about on his own.

At last the rehearsal was over and Miss Fisher bundled them off the school premises. As usual they all wandered back to Maggie's house. She was the only one who had to get back and the others enjoyed being with her. The rehearsal had been a late one and it was already beginning to get dark. Just then they heard the distant ee-awing of a police siren. They looked round excitedly as it got nearer and nearer, the flashing blue light whirling round and round. The glare of headlights blinded them as the police car sped past.

"I wonder what's up," said Leo.

"A punch-up, I expect," said Fred hopefully.

"Probably a drunk," remarked Alan. "It's a bit early though. The pubs haven't been open for long."

"I just don't understand why people get drunk," said Maggie casually. There was a sudden silence and her face reddened. She'd forgotten that they'd all seen Leo's dad drunk more than once.

Surprisingly, it was Leo himself who put them at ease. "It can't be my dad this time," he said cheerfully. "He's just started a job as night watchman."

"I bet someone's been coshed," said Fred. "They're always doing it round here. Soon there won't be anyone left who hasn't been coshed."

"You don't half talk a load of rubbish," Leo said. "Of course it doesn't go on all the time."

Fred swayed along the kerb clutching his head in a realistic manner and chanted, "I've been coshed, properly coshed, horrible . . ."

Maggie looked at him severely. "Stop it, Fred," she said so sharply that Fred did stop it. "You're just being stupid. It's not even funny. You ought to be ashamed of . . ."

"Maggie!" Alan had reached the corner first. There was an anxious look on his face. "Maggie! The police are outside your house."

"Mum and Bobby!" Maggie's face was white. Without another word she pelted up the road, the boys hard on her heels. She bounded up the front steps and practically fell into the arms of a young policeman who was standing just inside the door. "What's wrong?" she panted. "Where's mum and Bobby? What's happened?"

"You live here, do you?"

She nodded. "Where's Mum? What's happened?" and she tried to push past him.

He held her gently by the arm. "Calm down, young lady," he said. "Nobody's been hurt. You can see your mother in a moment."

Tears sprang into Maggie's eyes. "What's happened to her? I want to see my Mum."

"Can't she go in?" asked Alan.

"Not till the fingerprint men have finished," said the

125

constable. "They won't be long." He looked at Maggie's face. Tears were rolling down it. He handed her a handkerchief. "Wipe your eyes. You don't want to upset your mother, do you?" Maggie shook her head and sniffed.

"Please," she said. "Let me in."

At last there was movement inside and three policemen came out. "Who's this?" asked one.

"I'm Maggie and I want my Mum," she shouted.

"Come along then," he said, and Maggie rushed in. Her mother was standing just inside the kitchen and Maggie threw herself into her arms. "There isn't much more we can do, Mrs Hobbs," he said. "I do want you to have a good look round, and if you find anything missing at all, no matter how trivial it seems, make a note and let us know. Perhaps you'll come down to the station tomorrow and make a statement. Good night, Mrs Hobbs. Good night, Maggie. I do hope the tidying up won't take too long."

The police got into their car and drove away while the constable stayed behind to move on the usual crowd of spectators. The boys hung around for a few moments hoping that Maggie would come out and tell them all about it, but eventually they too went home.

By this time Maggie and her mother had made a cup of tea and were sitting together in the middle of almost unbelievable chaos. Mrs Hobbs still had a look of habitual calm on her thin face. Although she had had to work for years to bring up her family on her own after her husband died, she always managed to sound placid and controlled. "Just our luck it should happen when you were out, Maggie," she said. "It might not have happened at all if you had been here."

"What did happen?" asked Maggie. "Tell me right from the beginning."

"Well," began her mother, "I was upstairs putting Bobby

126

to bed when the money ran out. One minute it was bright and the next it was dark. I found my handbag and began to go through it for some change and, of course, I couldn't find any. I'd only got pound notes and some small coins. Bobby didn't seem to mind, he was half-asleep anyway, so I just sat there enjoying the peace and quiet for a moment and I thought I'd sent you out for some change when you got home. Once I did think I heard the door go, but then I didn't hear anything else so I thought I'd imagined it. I must have been sitting there for quite a long time when I heard a funny noise. I called out 'Is that you, Maggie?' and then there was a crash and then a man coughed. Well, I knew that couldn't be you, so I put Bobby down very carefully and I picked up that big brass jug and went downstairs . . ."

"Mum," breathed Maggie, "How did you dare?"

Her mother smiled and ruffled her hair. "I wasn't that brave, Maggie," she said. "To tell you the truth I made quite a lot of noise. I wasn't really very keen on meeting him, and it didn't seem that he was very keen on meeting me, because before I was half-way down the door was slammed hard and when I got out onto the steps there was no one in sight at all. He'd just vanished. So I just popped into Mrs Jones and asked her to telephone the police and I borrowed some change at the same time and came back to this."

They both looked at the hideous mess around them. Drawers had been emptied, their contents strewn about, and cupboards had been searched. Everything in the sideboard had been tossed contemptuously onto the pile, cushions had been ripped open and two of the chairs were upside down.

"I must say I got a bit of a shock when I saw all this. I had a good look round, of course, but the funny thing is, there doesn't seem to be anything missing at all. He didn't even take the rent money, and that was just sitting on the shelf. I

127

can't think what he was after. I can only think he made a mistake."

Maggie started collecting together the socks and putting them in one pile. "Fancy breaking into a house where there were people, though. I mean, it seems mad."

"He might not have thought anyone was here, Maggie," said her mother, sorting through the papers that had been thrown about. "You see I only had the light on for a couple of ticks before it went out and then I was sitting in the dark. So perhaps it did look deserted. The funny thing is, it nearly was. I was in the fish shop this morning with Mrs Jones when I heard that poor old Mr Andrews who lives alone was ill. So I said that I'd go and sit with him this evening, and Mrs Jones said that she'd have Bobby and take you in when you got home. But later on I heard that the poor old chap had been taken to hospital, so I didn't go out after all."

Maggie picked up the cups and took them out to the sink. She stood at the door to the kitchen and looked at the confused heap of clothes and books and papers, at the stuffing from the cushions that had been thrown about and at the broken chairs. "Oh, Mum," she said, "what a mess. We'll never get it cleaned up."

"It won't take long just to tidy it," said her mother cheerfully. "We can sort it out properly another time, but we'll get it straight in no time at all if we go at it together. We can keep our eyes open at the same time and see if anything's missing."

She was quite right. It didn't take nearly as long as Maggie had thought it would to make the place look fairly tidy. Maggie straightened herself up at last. "Isn't it funny," she said. "I don't think anything's been taken at all? Do you want anything else done, Mum?"

"No, that's lovely, Maggie," said her mother. "You look

dead tired, lovey. You'll be properly washed out tomorrow. I think you'd better go to bed."

Maggie looked at her pleadingly. "Have I got to, Mum? Can't I stay up with you a bit longer. I don't really feel tired and I know I won't sleep."

"All right, but only for a few minutes," said her mother. "You haven't told me yet how the play went."

Maggie brightened up. "It's getting ever so good," she said. "We're going to try our costumes on tomorrow. I've got a white dress with gold on the sleeves and round the neck, but I've got to find something to put on my head. Miss Fisher did think of the crown we had in the Christmas play but she thinks it's too big and heavy for me now. She thinks I ought to have something more like a little circlet or something in my hair. Can you think of anything, mum?"

Her mother pursed her lips and thought over the few little bits of imitation jewellery they had. "What about that string of beads Aunt Alice gave me?" she suggested. "They're not much good for anything else, but they might look all right from a distance since they're that cheap glittery glass. If we put your hair up and threaded the beads in and out it might look quite pretty."

"Could we try it now, Mum?" Without waiting for an answer Maggie jumped to her feet, gave her mother a quick hug and clattered upstairs. She tiptoed into her mother's room since Bobby was fast asleep in there and rummaged around in the box where they kept their odds and ends. She found the beads, hastily picked up a comb and brush and a handful of hairpins, took a quick look at Bobby, who was sleeping in a neat little bundle, and hurried downstairs again.

She sat on the floor at her mother's feet while Mrs Hobbs brushed and combed her dark hair and swept it up on the top of her head. Her mother looked at it critically and then let it fall down and tried again. Eventually she managed to pin it up to her own satisfaction and then she looked at Maggie. "Why, Maggie," she said in surprise, "you look quite pretty."

Maggie blushed. "Oh, come of it, Mum," she mumbled. But she had an expression of delight on her face; she was as unused to compliments from her mother, as her mother was unused to paying them.

Her mother carefully entwined the long string of cheap beads in Maggie's hair. "There you are," she said at last. "Go and see what you think."

Maggie jumped and hurried over to the mantlepiece to stare at her reflection. A happy smile spread over her face, and she turned her head first one way and then the other in an effort to get a better look. "Gosh!" she said at last. "You're a marvel. It doesn't look like me at all."

Impulsively she turned and rushed to give her mother a kiss, but her foot caught the edge of the rug and she stumbled and fell on the floor with a crash. Her hair tumbled down and the beads fell out. As she got up she stepped on several of them and they crunched into hundreds of tiny pieces. "Oh, Mum," she cried, tears rolling down her cheeks, "I've spoiled them."

Her mother got up and gave her a quick squeeze. "Never mind, ducky," she said comfortingly. "You've done me a good turn. I never liked them. You've never seen me wear them, have you?" Maggie shook her head. "Let's pick up those that are all right and we'll have a good look at them tomorrow. There might be enough for us to string together and if there aren't we'll see what we can do. There are plenty of cheap ones in the market, so you needn't worry about that. Don't cry, lovey. Come and help me."

Maggie rubbed the tears from her eyes, feeling a bit ashamed of behaving like a baby, and started to crawl around picking up as many beads as she could. Her mother put them all into a little box and placed it carefully on the shelf. "Now up you go," she said firmly. "It's much too late to do anything more tonight. Hurry, Maggie. There's no need to hang round my neck looking like a dying duck in a thunderstorm, because it won't make any difference. You'll still have to go to bed."

Maggie took a quick look at her mother's face. Delaying tactics would be useless, she decided, so she rubbed her nose up and down her mother's cheek. "Good night, mum," she said. "It was lovely staying up with you, even if it was only because of the burglar." She gave her mother a final kiss and went off happily to bed.

CHAPTER EIGHT

Marie managed to persuade her mother to let her go to schoo
the following day, though not without difficulty. Mrs Jenkin
chose to see Marie as a nervous, highly strung girl, instead o
the tough, resilient one she really was. Once back, however
she found she was not enjoying it at all. The maths lesson wa
hideous. She couldn't get anything right at all, and sh
scowled furiously when the teacher said that those in th
play were to go into the hall after break instead of havin
ordinary lessons. He glanced at Marie. "What's wrong wit
you?" he asked. "Still feeling unwell, or is this a demon
stration of the famous Jenkins temper?"

Most of the class turned round to stare and Marie wen
bright red. "I'm all right," she muttered, and as he went ou
of the room she buried her head in her desk and pretended t
be looking for a book.

"Are you really all right?" hissed Maggie.

"Mind your own business," snapped Marie.

Maggie's temper flared up. "All right," she said angril
"from now on I'll do just that. As far as I'm concerne
you're just not here, you don't exist, you're nothing!"

Stimulated by the thought of a good row, Marie slamme
the lid of her desk down as loudly as possible and turned t

face Maggie. "If I'm nothing you're . . . "

"Marie Jenkins!" Mr Marsh was in the room glaring at her. "You are undoubtedly the most garrulous girl it has been my misfortune to teach. I am never able to come into a room without finding you chattering away like a monkey." Marie glared at him, but under his steady gaze she finally dropped her eyes. She knew better than to cross swords with him and so she tried to appear utterly absorbed in what he was saying.

"Open your text books at page thirty. We will see how much you have remembered, or perhaps it would be more accurate to say we will see how much you have forgotten. Look at the first sentence and put up your hands if you can tell me what is wrong with it."

Marie looked blankly at the sentence. It seemed all right to her, but as other hands shot up all round her she raised hers too so that she wouldn't look conspicuous and trusted to luck that she wouldn't be asked.

As the lesson droned on she became more and more bored, and whilst keeping an attentive face turned towards Mr Marsh she switched her mind towards her grievances. Her friends, she decided, had simply turned against her and that was all there was to it. Well, let them. They would be the ones who would regret it, not she. When they returned, and she was sure they would, seeking her friendship, they would find things were very different. She smiled slightly at the thought of what she would say to them. Mr Marsh brought her back to reality with a jolt.

"Well," he said sarcastically, "and just what is your valuable opinion, Marie? We have all been waiting for some time with bated breath to hear it."

Marie looked at him with loathing. She hadn't the slightest idea what he was on about, and she knew that he knew she didn't. She cast her eyes down. "I don't know, Mr Marsh," she said meekly.

"You don't know!" he repeated in mock surprise. "You don't know! Could it be that you were not listening?" He shook his head sadly and the class watched the pantomime with pleasure. "Now you have spoiled my day for me. The only thing that has kept me going is the thought of your tremendous enthusiasm." His voice hardened. "Unless you can keep up some semblance of interest I'm afraid Marie, that I might be forced to spoil your day for you."

"Rotten old pig!" said Marie to herself, but she concentrated on the lesson for the rest of the period. She sighed with relief when the bell went for break at last and she had escaped without even being put in detention.

In the playground Fred, completely forgetting that they were all going to leave her to get over it on her own, joined her. "We've just had P.T.," he groaned. "We had to keep on having races over the horse and up the ropes, and every time I went past Mr May he shouted 'Come on, Dobbin' and my team lost and I'm getting the blame as usual." He chattered on, cheerfully unaware that Marie was deliberately taking no notice. "Then Mr May made us hang upside down on the wall-bars and I hate that. It takes me ages to get up and by the time I'm up everybody else is down. And when I did get down they'd picked up sides for basketball so I got left out. It's rotten, isn't it?" Marie went on staring into the distance.

Leo came over and joined them. He knew he was supposed to leave Marie alone, but he hated being bad friends with anyone. "How are you, Marie?" he asked. "I'm surprised your Mum let you come back to school so soon. Maggie said you still looked a bit rough."

"That *was* kind of her," said Marie sarcastically as she moved away.

Leo looked meaningly at Fred and shrugged his shoulders. "I guess Alan's right," he said. "She'll just have to get over it on her own."

Fred looked at Marie, who was now standing alone in the centre of the playground. "Is something up?" he asked, puzzled. "I though she was ever so chatty."

The bell went and they all trooped in for the rest of morning school. From her classroom Marie could hear muffled sounds coming from the hall. There was the sound of trampling feet over and over again and then the despairing of "Fred!" and "Take him outside, Alan." A few minutes later their heads bobbed past the window. By craning her neck Marie could just see them in the playground. Alan shouted commands and Fred, a look of grim determination on his face, slouched past in what he obviously considered a military manner. "Left turn!" sent him swinging off to the right. "Slope arms!" meant in Fred's terms "Drop your rifle on the ground and fall over it." As time went on the look of determination faded and was replaced by a particularly maddening grin that obviously brought Alan close to screaming pitch. Marie watched it all with malicious pleasure until, much to her regret, they disappeared round the corner and she could barely hear their voices.

At lunch time, although it was completely forbidden, Marie slipped out of school. She knew she couldn't bear to sit at the same table as the others and hear them going on and on about the play. So she went straight to the fish and chip shop and joined the long queue that moved slowly up to the counter. She was standing directly behind two women who were gossiping excitedly together. She pricked up her ears and edged a little closer to them as soon as she realised they were talking about a burglary that had happened in the neighbourhood.

135

"You could wake up any day," said one seriously, "and find you'd had your throat cut in the night. It's not good enough."

"It's not good enough," echoed her friend, nodding so that the dejected feathers on her hat danced with some animation. "That's what I say. It's not good enough. Nobody's safe these days. All you hear is talk, talk, talk, and what do they do to protect us, that's what I'd like to know? What do they do?"

"Nothing! They just don't care. Do you know it took the police five minutes to get there? And what did they find? I'll tell you. Nothing. That's what they found. He'd gone. Just walked out as easy as kiss your hand. I expect he was in the local having a quiet pint while the police were still on the way. It really is disgusting!"

The feathers trembled as the heads got closer together. "What did he get away with?"

"Everything, poor soul. The rent, the telly, her bag, the lot! He stripped it, completely stripped it." Marie longed to say that the thief having a quiet pint might have looked a bit conspicuous with a television set under his arm but she kept quiet. "And there was that poor little kid in bed all the time. Lucky he was asleep if you ask me or who knows what might have happened to him."

"Poor kid!"

"And do you think the police have caught him yet? Of course they haven't. They're far too busy waiting round turnings trying to catch my Stan when he's got to rush a lorry load to the docks."

"It must have given Mrs Hobbs a nasty turn, mustn't it?"

For a moment or two Marie had lost interest in what they were saying, but the name snapped her back into immediate consciousness. "Did you say Mrs Hobbs?" she demanded.

The women turned round. "That's right. Why, do you know her?"

Marie bit her lip. "Yes!" she said. She suddenly rushed out of the shop and back into the school and burst into the dining-room. Fortunately the teacher on duty was in the kitchen and so didn't see Marie as she flung her arms round Maggie's neck. "Maggie!" she cried. "Your poor mum! What's she going to do? You ought to have told me. Fancy having everything stolen!"

Maggie dropped her spoon in astonishment. The last time they'd spoken Marie had been really nasty and now here she was with her arms round her neck. "What are you talking about?"

"The woman in the fish and chip shop said you'd been burgled and that he got away with everything."

"Oh, that. Well, we were upset last night because of the mess and everything, but somehow it didn't seem so bad this morning."

Marie slipped into her accustomed place. "But what happened?"

"Some nut, at least he must have been a nut to break into any house in our street, got in while mum was upstairs with Bobby and started pulling the whole place to pieces. She heard him and called out, but by the time she'd got downstairs he'd gone. It was funny though because he didn't take anything, not even the money on the shelf. The police came but mum said she couldn't imagine how they could find anything out. There weren't even any fingerprints."

"But no one would have broken in for nothing," Leo pointed out.

"Maggie's mum makes super bread pudding," said Fred reflectively. They all ignored him.

"I don't suppose he specially picked our house," said

137

Maggie. "It just looked empty. The funny thing is that i
nearly was." And she told them how her mother had planne(
to go and sit with old Mr Andrews and she and Bobby wer(
to sleep next door.

Marie's eyes sparkled. "There you are then," she sai(
triumphantly. "Anyone could have heard what was said ii
the fish shop. I bet old Harbottle was snooping around an(
took his chance."

"Yes, but his chance to do what?" asked Alan. "Honestly
Marie, you've got such a thing about him that if you just sav
him asking the time you'd think he was planning to steal th(
crown jewels."

"He probably would be," said Marie complacently.

"We haven't got anything he could possibly want," sai(
Maggie, "not unless he wanted to break open the electri(
meter, and he didn't go near that."

"Perhaps he was after Bobby's puppet," said Fred. The
all roared with laughter.

"Perhaps he wanted Maggie's old teddy-bear," suggeste(
Leo and they all roared again.

"You are stupid sometimes, Fred," said Maggie. "Onl
someone who'd got a screw loose would want a thing lik
that."

"Or someone who collected them," whispered Leo t
Fred. "We mustn't forget to go to Bernie's."

"What about Saturday," said Fred doubtfully. "I suppos
there would be time before the play?"

Marie pulled a long face. "I won't half be glad when th
play's over," she said. "It feels like it's lasted a year alread y
You never have time for anything else now. I suppose you'v
got another rehearsal tonight and I'll be left on my ow
again."

Alan looked slightly guilty. "As a matter of fact we have,

he admitted. "Miss Fisher wants us to go all the way through it without a break."

Maggie beamed and clutched Marie's arm. "I've got it!" she exclaimed. "Fred's not in the first scene so he can be with you. Then Alan can slip out because he's not wanted in the second scene, and then you can have Fred again. Then we can all go home to my place and have tea together."

"Lovely," said Marie happily.

"What about your mother, Marie?" asked Alan. "Unless you let her know you're going to be late she'll have the whole of the police force looking for you."

"I'll get Rose Forster to tell her," said Marie. "She goes past our house every day."

Within a few minutes they were back in school for afternoon lessons. The girls had cookery, which they enjoyed, so the time seemed to pass quickly. They came out with their arms entwined and munching each other's biscuits. Maggie went straight into the hall and Marie joined Fred, who was waiting for her, propped up against the wall.

"Have one," she said, holding out the bag.

He put it straight into his mouth. "What shall we do?" he mumbled indistinctly, crumbs spilling from the sides of his mouth.

"Don't speak with your mouth full," said Marie severely. "I was going to say we could dash home to my house and have a cup of tea, but my mum wouldn't give you one if she saw the way you stuffed food into yourself."

Fred gulped it down. "Sorry," he said. "It seemed a bit on the small side."

Marie took the hint and passed the bag over again. This time Fred nibbled genteelly at it. "Shall we go there then?" he asked.

"There isn't much time," said Marie. "Maggie said we'd

only got about twenty minutes. Still, we can if we hurry."

Fred halted. "I don't want to be late," he said. "Miss Fisher will be mad at me again if I am."

"There won't be time if you crawl along like that," said Marie impatiently. "Anyway, I'll listen to your lines as we go along."

Fred halted once again. He pointed stiffly to the left. "Ho!" he exclaimed. He shaded his eyes with his other hand and stared into the distance. "See, she comes!" He bowed awkwardly, one hand on his heart, the other still shading his eyes. "Your Highness!" he bellowed.

"You look as if you're stark raving mad," said Marie. "I'm not taking you home if you carry on like this. My mum wouldn't like it."

Fred had a hurt expression on his face as he straightened up. "They're my lines," he said, wounded. "You told me to say my lines and I didn't get them wrong this time. At least, I don't think I did." He began to mutter them over and over again to himself.

"Fred!" said Marie sharply, jabbing him in the ribs. "Belt up. People are beginning to look at you. You look as if you're round the bend, shooting up your arm and doubling over like that."

Marie wasn't exaggerating. Fred was being stared at by a number of people, and some went out of their way to avoid him, one even stepping into the gutter. Seeing one curious face after another fastened on him, Fred straightened up and tried to be nonchalant and promptly walked into a lampost.

"Oh, what a fool!" cried Marie furiously.

Fred grasped the lampost. "Hi!" he shouted.

Marie groaned. "For crying out loud, Fred, can't you even remember your lines? It's 'Ho!' not 'Hi!.' Come on. Stop messing about!"

He gripped the lampost tightly with one hand and pointed with his right one in a dramatic gesture. Marie pushed his arm down and thrust out the other one. "Use your left one," she said. "You're not very good at remembering, are you?"

Fred pushed her hand away and pointed with his right one again. "Hi!" he repeated. "Look who's coming!"

Marie put her hands on her hips. "See she comes," she said patiently, with the air a nurse might use on a particularly backward and difficult patient. "See she comes."

"Not she, he," shouted Fred.

"Don't be so silly. You said it was she."

"What on earth are you gabbling about?" asked Fred, his eyes fixed on something on the other side of the road. "How can a man be a girl? Look, he's over there with another man right by the dairy. The one who buys puppets, I mean."

"Is he?" Marie glanced up and looked casually across the road. She looked harder. Her eyes glittered. "That's Harbottle!" she exclaimed, and grabbed Fred's hand in her excitement. "I wonder who he's talking to?"

"I suppose he's talking to Harbottle," said Fred uneasily. He wanted Marie to let his hand go but didn't like to say so.

"Wait a minute," Marie groaned. "Harbottle's wearing the grey cap. You haven't seen him before, have you?"

Fred wriggled. He managed to free one finger. "No, but the guy in the suit with the glasses is the one who tried to buy Bobby's puppet. He's the one who's a collector. I thought perhaps he was called Harbottle." He succeeded in freeing his hand, and he held it carefully in the other so that Marie shouldn't have a chance of grabbing it again.

Marie looked thoughtful. "They must be in it together then."

"In it? In what?" Fred hadn't actually followed her line of thought.

"In this plot," she said impatiently, and reached for his hand. Fred hastily put them both behind his back. "Quick!" she said. "Let's hide behind the pillar box. I don't think they've spotted us yet and we can keep an eye on them from here." She dragged him round and then peered out cautiously. "It's all right. They can't have seen us. They're still talking to each other."

"What plot?" asked Fred. He didn't really mind being hauled about by Marie, but he was a bit put out by her talk of a plot. The only plot he was conscious of was the one in the play, and he found it all a bit confusing. "How do I know?" snapped Marie. "That's what I'm trying to find out, thick head."

"But what . . . . ?"

"Sh! They're moving. We'll have to follow them." She dragged Fred from behind the pillar box and started to trail them. She tried to keep them in sight without getting too close, and so their progress was a series of scurried little rushes as the men unexpectedly hurried or halted. This resulted in their banging into a number of people, who either grumbled or pushed past them. Marie, however, was so intent on her quarry that she hardly noticed. Now and again one of the men looked round and Marie gave Fred a quick shove into the shelter of a shop doorway or into a queue, and crossed her fingers hoping that they hadn't been spotted.

"Where are we going?" Fred asked occasionally as he was pulled and pushed and shoved from one place to another.

Marie didn't bother to answer. How could she? She hadn't the slightest idea of what was going to happen either. As they got further down the market the crowds thinned and it became more and more difficult for them to hide and the men seemed to look round more and more frequently.

Marie used anything for cover and so they hid behind a

dustcart, and she even shoved him down the basement of a wine merchant's, so quickly that he almost fell down a steep narrow flight of stairs. She tugged him into an alley where they hid behind a dustbin, and then, after taking a quick look round, crept out into the street again.

Suddenly Marie almost pulled him over. "Here!" she hissed, and thrust him under a barrow, where they had to squat among some rotten fruit.

As they crouched together Fred turned to her, a worried frown on his face. "What's the time, Marie? I mustn't be late." Marie took no notice of him. She was far too busy peering from beneath the fringe of green imitation grass that covered the stall and hung down over the front and the sides. She could just see the legs of the two men, who had come to a halt no more than five yards away. They stood and whispered excitedly together.

"Marie," said Fred plaintively, "I'll be late if I don't go and Miss Fisher might give my lines to someone else. Mind you, I don't suppose anyone else could learn them in time, not properly." He tried to stand upright and cracked his head on the underside of the stall. "Ouch!" he said loudly and rubbed his head vigorously.

"Sh! You'll give us away."

Fred held his head in both of his arms. "Well, it hurts," he protested. "If it was your head . . ."

"Shut up! I'm trying to listen," she whispered.

Harbottle and his friend marched briskly towards the stall and stopped close to the green curtain. "O.K. then," said Harbottle, loudly and clearly. "I'll keep my eyes skinned for one. There isn't much time left though, is there?"

"Everything's under control, my dear fellow, so let's not panic. I'm not sure that I'll actually be able to see you tomorrow, since I've got one or two things to attend to here and there and I really must try to pop into that exhibition again before it closes. I'll get in touch with you if I find I need you." Marie thought how pleasant this man's voice was. It was fairly deep and cultured and had an amused quality about it that she found really rather attractive.

"All right then, Guv." And Harbottle's legs moved off while the gleaming shoes and well-pressed trousers of the other man stayed exactly where they were.

Marie put her mouth to Fred's ear. "Harbottle doesn't know you," she breathed. "Follow him and don't let him catch you." Fred began to slither from under the barrow. "Not that way, stupid. You'll be spotted."

Fred crawled out on his hands and knees and picked himself up. Suddenly his face, partly covered with the green cloth, so that he looked a bit like a half-hearted monster, reappeared. "What about my part then?" Marie looked at him in disgust and picked up a squashed tomato in a threatening way. Fred shrunk back. "All right, all right. I was only asking," he said, withdrawing his head once more.

Marie hardly noticed once he had gone. She was far too busy watching a pair of well-shod feel advancing on the stall. She moved back among the mouldy oranges and rotten pears as silently as possible. The feet halted. Marie stared at them as if hypnotised. Suddenly the green cloth was whipped up and a tanned face peered down at her. "So we meet at last," said the amused voice.

Marie glared up at him belligerently. She felt humiliated at being discovered in this way. "I don't know what you mean," she said. "I don't want to meet you particularly."

The man's face fell. "How terribly disappointing," he said. "I was rather looking forward to it. It's really some time since a young lady has shown interest in me and you can't imagine how dull it is to get older and older and to know that probably they never will again." '

Marie's blue eyes flickered up and down him and then she stared him straight in the eye. "I don't suppose they will," she said rudely.

Much to her surprise he roared with laughter. "I asked for that in a way," he said and smiled at her again. "Actually I was counting on your sympathy. I thought you would think how sad it was and creep from under that grubby little curtain and talk to me."

"I don't want to talk to you."

He waggled a reproving finger at her and shook his head. "Come on now. Tell the truth. You know you're longing to know all about me."

Marie's cheeks went faintly pink but she said airily enough, "I can't imagine what made you think that. I just happened to be going the same way as you."

"Oh, come, come, that really won't do. You made a pretty good job of shadowing us, but I'm afraid your companion simply wasn't in the same class as you. He just isn't skilful enough. To tell you the truth we were aware of him for some little time, which was how we managed to spot you in the end." Marie tucked that piece of information away for future use. "Besides," he went on, "we have an advantage over you. You see, we know your name. It's Mata Hari, I believe." Marie remained silent. His head disappeared for a moment and then it popped back. He stuck his hand underneath the barrow. "However, that's something we can remedy. Here, take this," and he proffered a small white card.

Marie regarded it suspiciously. "What is it?" she asked, holding it gingerly as though it was a stick of dynamite.

"It's my card. It's got my name and address on it. I thought it might help to convince you that I am an ordinary law-abiding citizen, with no evil designs on you." His voice became pleading. "Now do come out. My back is aching and it's no joke at my age. What is more, I know I will get a frightful headache if I have to spend any more time upside down. I wasn't actually brought up to be a bat."

Marie looked down at the card. "What's your name then?" she demanded truculently.

He smiled at her. "You won't catch me like that, though I must say you're very wise to check the facts. My name's exactly what it says on the card. I'm Major Graham and I live in Cumberland. I'll give you the full address if you want me to."

"You're a long way from home then, aren't you?"

"At the moment I am staying in a friend's flat until I can find one of my own. I do live in the country most of the time but it's useful to have somwhere permanent to park oneself in London instead of having to book in at hotels. You know, I can see you don't want to believe me, but honestly I truly am nothing but a completely harmless ordinary man. Is there anything else you would like to know about me?"

Marie looked directly at him. "Yes, there is. If you're what you say you are then what are you doing with a man like Harbottle who sometimes calls himself Smith?"

The Major looked astounded. He poked his head further under the green cloth and stared at her. "Are you sure — absolutely sure? I mean, you're not joking or anything like that?" Marie shook her head. "Good gracious!" He pulled out a neatly-folded handkerchief and mopped his brow. "But I have known him for years. I can't believe he uses an alias. What would he do that for? There can't be some mistake, can there?" He looked anxiously at Marie's face and sighed. "No, I see there can't. Well, that certainly helps to explain why you're so suspicious of me. We must have seemed like birds of a feather to you."

Marie edged forward a little more. She still didn't trust him, but certainly his astonishment seemed genuine enough to her. "Just what are you after?" she asked. "Is it that doll?" The Major nodded, a slightly ashamed look on his face. "I can hardly believe it," she said slowly, "not a grown man like you playing with dolls."

"It's not exactly playing with dolls," protested the Major. "It's not like that at all." He put his hand to his back and groaned slightly. "Are you quite sure I can't persuade you to come out?" he asked pathetically. "It's all right at your age but believe me, at mine it's absolute hell."

Marie was a bit sick of the smell of over-ripe fruit herself. "All right then," she said, trying to make it sound as if she was bestowing a great favour on him. "If it makes it a bit easier for you I will." Trying hard to look dignified, she edged out and stood stiffly in front of him.

The Major straightened up slowly and rubbed his hands up and down his back as far as he could reach. "That's better," he said at last. "I was afraid I might be stuck like that for ever," and he smiled again at her. Marie remained silent, her face immobile. He rubbed his chin thoughtfully and then started polishing his glasses. He put them on and gave her a sharp look. "I can see you're a business-like young lady," he said, "and it will be no good beating about the bush with you. Now where shall we go for our little chat? Is there a coffee bar round here? Or would you like to wait until your friends join us?"

Actually she was terribly thirsty, but she wasn't giving an inch. "I don't want a little chat with you," she said. "I don't know what makes you think I do. And anyway my friends can't come. They're still in school rehearsing."

To Marie's surprise the Major sounded interested. "What

are they doing?" he asked. "I used to be very keen on the theatre."

Suddenly Marie found herself chattering to him with great enthusiasm about the plot and the scenery and how the performance was going to be in the school hall on Saturday.

"You'll be there?" he asked.

Marie's eyebrows shot up. "Of course I will," she said emphatically. It had never occurred to her not to go.

"How silly of me," he said. "What a fool I must sound. Of course you will be there. You must be in it. I imagine you are the princess."

Marie tried to sound indifferent. "As a matter of fact, I'm not," she said casually. "Maggie is. She's ever so good and she sings better than me."

The Major raised one eyebrow and then shrugged his shoulders. "Well, quite frankly, you astound me. It's not that I doubt your friend's ability in the slightest, but surely you look much more the part. I thought it was practically a rule for all stage princesses to have fair hair and blue eyes just like you." Marie remained silent. She thought so, too, but she wasn't going to give him the satisfaction of agreeing with him. "I imagine it's frightfully dull for you with all your friends in it," he said understandingly. "You must get terribly bored. There must be someone who's not got a part though. What about that little boy? Maggie's brother, isn't it? Is he a page, or is he just going to be one of the audience like you?"

Marie frowned. She didn't care to be put in the same category as Bobby. "He's got to be in the audience whether he likes it or not, because there certainly won't be anyone to look after him at home," she said. "I don't have to go unless I want to. I can please myself." She began to twist a wisp of hair round her finger. "Actually I haven't made up my mind one way or the other yet. Anyway, I'm not going to sit next to him and his stinking puppet. He's sure to take it with him." She bit her lip and shot a glance at the Major to see if he was offended by her description of the puppet. He appeared not to have noticed. He was polishing his glasses once again.

"When did you say the play is?" he asked casually. "I must have a mind like a sieve. You did tell me, I know."

"Saturday. Why?"

"No reason at all except curiosity, I suppose. Now what about that cup of coffee? It would be much pleasanter to have a chat over one than standing by this smelly old barrow."

"Why don't you give up?" said Marie firmly. "There's nothing I want to talk to you about and anyway I haven't time to hang around, even if you have."

The major looked a bit disappointed. "Now we know you were not following me around just because you liked my looks," he said. "We have already established that. Come on," he said coaxingly, "be honest. Admit you are just the tiniest bit curious about me."

"You're not my type at all." Actually she was beginning to find that she quite enjoyed talking to him. He seemed astonishingly understanding and sympathetic, but still, she reminded herself sternly, he still had a fair amount of explaining to do.

"Oh, well," the Major said, "if you won't come that's just my bad luck. But you know, I'm still a tiny bit puzzled. I can see you still don't really trust me and I can't see why. I have given you my name and address. It's true I can't describe my job to you, because the truth is I don't have one. I'm one of the fortunate ones, I suppose. I have just about enough money to keep myself ticking over without having to work. What else can I tell you?"

Marie looked directly at him. "I asked you once. You didn't answer properly. If you're so respectable why do you knock around with Harbottle?"

The Major threw back his head and laughed. "My dear girl, you appear to have Harbottle on the brain. I find him useful, that's all. He does errands for me and since I spend a fair amount of time south of the river he keeps his eye open for the odd puppet. They still turn up from time to time, you know, and he is much better at driving a hard bargain than I am. The minute they see me coming they double their price. I must just look easy game."

"Then that's where they're wrong," said Marie shrewdly. "You might look soft but I reckon you're pretty tough. But you're wrong about Harbottle. I'm positive he's up to something right now and I wouldn't exactly fall backwards in surprise if I found out you knew all about it all the time."

The Major jabbed himself in the chest. "Me!" he said incredulously. "My dear girl, have you taken a close look at Harbottle? To tell the truth I find him slightly repulsive myself, so it's hardly surprising that you do. But really, does he exactly look like a crony of mine?"

Marie looked uncertain for the first time. That was one thing the Major was certainly right about. They were just not in the same class.

"I do assure you," the Major continued, "that although I hope I'm not a snob, he really isn't my sort of person." There was a convincing note in his voice and Marie began to regard him with a little less scepticism. He didn't notice her changed expression and went on. "I can tell it's no good. You've mentally tarred us with the same brush. If I could only find the right person to replace him I'd gladly give him the push."

He looked hard at Marie and a big smile spread across his face. "I've got it! I'll tell you what!" He lost his air of calm and looked quite excited. "Why don't you become my agent? It would be a damned sight more pleasant for me, I can tell you. After all, you are not only brighter, you are a great deal more attractive too. What about it? Would you take it on?"

"Would I take what on?" she asked, regarding him steadily. "You haven't offered me anything yet. All you've done is talk. What do you really mean?"

The Major drew a little nearer. "All right then," he said confidentially. "I'll make myself much clearer. At the risk of boring you, I'll remind you once again that I collect puppets. You are well aware of the fact that I want the one the little boy's got. In fact, I want it so much that I'm prepared to go up to twenty-five for it . . . ."

"Pounds?" asked Marie weakly.

"Yes, not guineas. The more I've thought about it the more I've decided I was a fool not to have offered more originally, but twenty-five is the absolute maximum. It really is the limit. As it is I shall have to spend a great deal of time repairing it, but if I can get it for that I shall be well satisfied. That fool Harbottle has been bungling around putting up everyone's back. I really don't know why he had to make it all seem such a cloak and dagger business."

"Do you want me to get Bobby to sell it to you?"

"That's exactly what I do mean," said the Major approvingly. "I felt sure I shouldn't have to spell things out to you. You see I feel absolutely certain that you will be able to find the right approach over something like this. If you can get hold of it for me I will pay you fifteen per cent. On anything else you find on your own, I will pay twenty."

"Fifteen per cent?" Marie's mind worked quickly. It seemed quite a lot of money.

"Fifteen per cent and not a penny more," said the Major. "So there's no point in trying to squeeze anything else out of me."

Marie looked at him dubiously. "Do you really mean it? You're not having me on?"

"Certainly not. I never joke about puppets or money, as you'll soon find out."

Marie looked down at her skirt, and seeing a bit of fluff clinging to it, she concentrated on pulling it off. "I'll think about it," she said casually.

"In that case I advise you not to take too long over it. That puppet is in a bad shape already, and unless I can begin restoring it pretty sharply, it won't be worth a brass farthing to anyone."

She smoothed down her skirt. "What about Harbottle then? Would you give him the sack like you said?"

"Oh, I think so. I would hardly need two people working the same area, would I? No, the minute you have made up your mind Harbottle will have to go. You know I have a funny feeling that we might work up quite a profitable association between us."

Marie stopped fiddling with her skirt at last. She looked searchingly at him. "You do want me to look out for other puppets, don't you?"

"Yes, and later on you might do a little bit of work on my other interests. Still, one thing at a time. The puppets come first."

Marie looked puzzled. "But I can't tell one puppet from another. How am I going to learn?"

The Major looked slightly bothered. "That's where Harbottle really is one up on you," he admitted. "He has been at this for some time now and he's almost as good as I am. Mark you, it's not that difficult, once you know what you're looking for." Then his face cleared and he smacked his hands together. "What an ass I am! There's a goodish little exhibition of puppets and dolls on at the moment. Why don't you pop along with me now? I could explain much more easily there because you'd actually have some to look at and examine. What do you say?"

Marie considered it. Almost all suspicion of the Major had evaporated. He sounded all right and he looked all right, and since he was going to give Harbottle the boot she supposed he really must be all right. "When?" she asked.

He grasped her elbow. "Now!" he said promptly. "My car's just round the corner. We could be there in a couple of ticks."

Marie shook herself free. "I can't go now," she said. "I told you I was waiting for my friends."

"So you did," said the Major ruefully. "What a memory I've got these days! I suppose you'll have to be at school for the rest of the week and I'm always busy in the evenings. Can't I persuade you to come on Saturday? It will have to be in the afternoon because I've got an appointment in the morning. I know it will mean missing the play, but does it really matter so much? It's the last day of the exhibition as it happens and it is much the best way for you to get the feel of the business." Marie stood there hesitantly. "Don't let me press you," he said easily. "If you think you ought not to let your friends down or they need you to help them to get dressed or to take care of the little boy, then it would be quite wrong of me to try to make you change your mind."

Marie squirmed at the thought of only being considered good enough to do the most menial jobs and so she shrugged her shoulders. "I'm not Maggie's dresser, if that's what you mean, and I'm not Bobby's keeper either. I didn't particularly want to go as it happens. After all, it's only a lot of kids dressing up."

"Well, that's wonderful," he said enthusiastically. "Let's meet at Kensington High Street underground station."

"When?"

"Well, when does the play start?"

"At three. But what's that got to do with it?"

"It will fix the time in your mind," the Major said. " mean, you are unlikely to forget when that is the very moment Maggie is setting foot on the stage."

"You needn't think I'll forget," said Marie decisively. "No that it would help me to remember anyway. I'm not really interested in the play. It all seems a bit childish somehow." She caught sight of the time. "Look at the time! I didn' know it was as late as that. I must go. I'll see you on Saturday at three." She flashed him a brilliant smile and turned to go.

"Wait a minute," he said. "Do you think you could have shot at getting hold of the puppet before then? If th wretched child should decide to part with it you could leav a message for me at this number," and he scribbled on th little card Marie was still holding. "I must say I would like t have it in my hands by Friday."

"Why Friday?" Marie asked sharply.

"Because it is the day before Saturday," he said quickly "Although it is almost unbelievably tatty I would just like t put it in the exhibition before it closes. It would be quite feather in my cap."

"You didn't say where the exhibition was," Marie pointe out.

"Nor did I. How stupid of me. It's Holland Park c course."

"But what if I don't get it for Friday?"

The Major shrugged. "It'll just be a pity, that's all. Anyway I will see you on Saturday whatever happens."

"Right," said Marie. "You don't need to worry about that smelly old doll. I'll get it one way or another, though it might take a bit of time."

She gave him a last quick smile and hurried off, feeling rather pleased with herself, although she was still faintly puzzled by the Major. Somehow he still didn't seem to be the sort of person who would be mad about puppets but then, she reflected, people hardly ever were what you thought they were. He had, however, been genuinely astounded about Harbottle, and he had been only too pleased at the idea of getting rid of him and taking her on instead. But that, she felt, was only as it should be. No, Harbottle, she decided, was simply up to something on his own and the Major was in the clear. She had been barking up the wrong tree there. There was nothing wrong with the Major except for his being cracked about puppets. Having come to that satisfactory decision she rushed on to her friends.

"Sorry I'm late," she said cheerfully. "I got held up."

"We've been hanging around for ages and we all kept running out when we weren't wanted on stage to see if you were there. Miss Fisher got really fed up with us," said Alan.

Fred poked her in the stomach. "I wasn't half late because of you," he said. "Miss Fisher said it was about time I learned to tell the time." He looked aggrieved and gave Marie another jab.

"Don't do that, Fred," said Maggie, "and of course Miss Fisher knows you can tell the time. She was a bit cross, that was all." Fred brightened up a bit.

"What did make you so late, Fred?" asked Leo curiously.

"I went after him like she said," Fred explained, "but he saw where I was hiding and he told me to clear off, so I did."

"Who did?"

"She did."

"You said . . . "

"Miss Fisher didn't tell you to clear off," said Maggie.

"No," Fred said. "I told you before. He did."

They all looked at each other wearily and much to Marie's relief they just let the matter drop.

"Let's go," said Maggie, walking in the direction of her house. But now that Fred had started on his story he wanted to finish it.

"You lot don't listen properly," he complained. "I was telling you all about this man that she said was up to no good. But I didn't really find anything out because he turned round and told me to clear off and so I was late."

"It doesn't matter now, Fred," said Marie quickly, steering him so that he was slightly ahead of the others.

"But don't you care?" he asked disconsolately, turning round to the rest of them. "I get back late, I miss my lines, I get jumped on by Miss Fisher and now you don't want to know."

"Never mind, Fred," said Maggie, moving up to join him. "You can say your lines to me on the way home if you like."

"Not likely," said Fred apprehensively. "Look what happened before."

"Hear mine then," said Leo.

Marie dropped back so that she was with Alan. "Do you think people really collect things like puppets and dolls?"

"Of course they do. People collect any old thing. You name it and they collect it. If you stop any kid at school his pocket will be full of things like stamps and matchboxes and stones and knives, and grown-ups are usually worse than kids."

Marie put her head closer to Alan's. "You know that chap

Harbottle," she began confidentially.

Alan groaned. "For crying out loud, Marie! It's about time you removed your bonnet and let that particular bee out. You'll go round the bend if you don't, and you'll probably take us with you."

Her face went pink with annoyance. "The trouble with you," she snapped, "is that you've got about the smallest mind in the world, so you can only take in teeny little things. Ever since you got in that stupid play . . . "

" . . . and ever since you didn't you've just run round and round in mad little circles. Can't you see what a fool you look?"

Marie pushed her way past him. "As if I care what you think! At least I've got myself a job while you lot have been rehearsing."

Alan caught at her hand. "What job? You'll tell me next you're a special agent," and he smiled at her in a superior way.

Marie jerked her arm free and ran up Maggie's steps. She stopped on the top one and looked down at him and smiled back in an equally superior way.

"Maybe I am," she said as she went in.

CHAPTER NINE

The next few days would have been almost unbearable for Marie had she not had the pleasure of looking forward to her trip with the Major. Everyone else was so wrapped up in the final preparations for the play that she felt completely out of things. Maggie was hardly ever in her classroom now and the others were often missing, even during break. Rehearsals and fittings for clothes seemed to go on continuously. Normally Marie would have felt aggrieved, as if the whole object of the play was to make her feel unwanted and unnecessary, but most of the time she hardly noticed what was going on for she was working out the best way of getting Bobby to part with his puppet.

At last, she made up her mind. She went up to Maggie. "I'll go and get Bobby after school for you," she said helpfully. "I know your mother's working late today and you'll all be needed here. I haven't really got anything else to do."

"Oh, Marie would you?" Maggie looked relieved. "I didn't like to ask."

"Fred could do it," said Leo.

"Don't be silly," said Marie. "Fred doesn't want to. He might be late again and you'd have to bring Bobby back here

nd he might be in the way. Anyway I heard Miss Fisher say
he didn't want Fred out of her sight again."

"She said something about not being able to rely on him,"
aid Leo, and then he clapped his hand to his mouth. He
adn't meant to let it out.

"Me! Can't rely on me!" cried Fred indignantly. "It wasn't
ay fault. It was hers," and he pointed at Marie. "I told you
he made me trail Harbottle."

Marie looked furious. "And a fat lot of good you were.
'ou were about as inconspicuous as an elephant."

"So that was why you were late," said Leo.

Marie was angry with herself as well as Fred. She hadn't
lanned on saying anything more about Harbottle or the
Iajor until she could wave a little wad of notes at them.

"Honestly," said Alan, "why don't we all shut up. All we
ver do is get across each other these days."

"Go on," said Marie, her eyes flashing, "go on, say it. Tell
nem it's me again, me and my temper, me and by obsession,
ae . . ."

"It's the play," said Maggie, "that's what it is. I'm
eginning to wish I wasn't in it. Of course it's rotten for
Iarie . . . "

"I don't mind, Maggie, really I don't," said Marie, and she
addenly realised she didn't. Somehow it had faded into
asignificance. "Look, I'll pick Bobby up like I said and take
im back to your house."

Fred had been turning over Marie's last remark to him.
I'm not," he said. "You're just getting at me again."

Marie turned to Maggie. "He's getting pretty quick these
ays, isn't he?"

Fred looked vaguely pleased at that and allowed himself to
e towed away by Maggie.

Immediately after afternoon school Marie hurried off to

fetch Bobby. He was waiting patiently by the school gate
singing a tuneless little song to himself. He looked up
suspiciously as Marie arrived. "Come on, Bobby" she said
brisky, "I'm taking you home today." She grasped his hand
and then withdrew it, a disgusted expression on her face. I
was unbelievably sticky. "What on earth have you been u
to?" she demanded. "Sweeping out a treacle factory?" Sh
took out her handkerchief and soaked it in the fountain b
the school gates. She rubbed his hands and her own whil
Bobby stood there quite placidly. He just went on singin
away as Marie led him along the road.

"I've been thinking about your puppet," she said. "Yo
don't really want it, do you? That man was right, you know
He said you could buy some with arms and legs that moved
I've been looking round the shops for you. There are som
smashing ones at Whiteley's. They've even got one that
dressed as a clown." She paused for a moment to see if sh
was having any effect at all, but since he was still chanting t
himself she couldn't tell whether he'd taken it in or no
"Would you like to come and see them?" she asked.

Bobby stood still and thought it over. He nodded. Mari
began to feel rather pleased with herself. The battle would b
virtually over, she thought, when he saw the new puppets. H
wasn't going to be interested in his old one after that. Sh
would be able to clinch the deal almost immediately. Sh
smiled inwardly as she imagined the Major's surprise whe
the phone rang that evening and he found she had pulled
off. She glanced down at Bobby. "I'm not sure when to tak
you though," she said. "The trouble is I can't go tomorro
and the play's on Saturday so we can't go then. It's a pit
really, because I don't think they'll have many left nex
week."

Bobby tugged at her hand until she looked down at him

He gazed up at her appealingly. She bent down to see what he wanted and he put his arms round her and whispered in her ear. Marie pretended to be surprised. "Now? I don't know about that, Bobby. It's a bit late, you know." Bobby stared up at her with unblinking eyes and Marie pretended to relent. "All right, then," she said. "We'll go now, but we'll have to get a move on. We'll go on a bus."

Hand in hand they ran back up the road, and they just managed to scramble on as it was drawing away from the bus stop. Within a few minutes they were entering the main doors of the shop. Marie, having already made one expedition there, knew exactly where to go, and she hustled Bobby through one department after another and into the lift and up to the toy department. Once there she let go of his hand.

There was a really magnificent display of puppets at the far end and Bobby ran down to them, clapping his hands together as he went. Then he came to a halt and stood completely still, entranced by them. There were witches on broomsticks with cats perched precariously on their shoulders, fairy-tale characters, soldiers and sailors, complete royal families together with haughty noblemen, knights in armour, a malicious monkey, a cheerful Mickey Mouse and everyone in 'Alice in Wonderland'. But as Marie had known from the first moment she had clapped eyes on them, it was the circus people that held Bobby's attention. He stood squarely in front of the ringmaster and sucked his thumb.

Marie let him look for several minutes before she grasped his hand and led him away. "Sorry, Bobby," she said to the back of his head, for he was still twisting round to catch a glimpse of them as they went through the doors. "I told you we couldn't stay long. I'd bring you back on Monday, but I don't think they'll have many left by then."

All the way home she talked to him about the puppets and

how you could make them move and dance, and all the time Bobby listened, a look of intense concentration on his face.

The second they got in she got Bobby his milk and biscuits and settled him down on the big chair and sat down on the arm of it. "Well," she said. "What about it? You'd like one of those, wouldn't ˙you?" Bobby nodded, his eyes shining. "Then run along and get your old one and I'll go straight to the man for you and bring back the money. I might even manage to go with you to the shop after school tomorrow." Bobby sat absolutely still. "Go on, silly," she said a little sharply. "You do want a new one, don't you?" Bobby nodded vigorously. "I thought you did. Now listen, you can't have a new one unless you give me your old one, so nip upstairs, or wherever you keep it, and bring it down to me."

Bobby stuck out his lower lip. Large tears appeared and hovered in the corner of his eyes. "Want new one," he quavered.

Marie took a deep breath. "Look, Bobby," she said, trying to keep her voice calm and patient, "those new ones cost lots and lots of money, and that nice man will give you lots and lots of money for your old one. Now do you understand?"

Bobby rubbed at the tears that were by now trickling down his face. "Want new one," he repeated.

Marie sighed heavily. "You can have one. All you've got to do is give me that nasty old one. Go on, there's a good boy."

Bobby shook his head violently. "No."

Marie got up and stood over him, her hands on her hips. "Oh, Bobby! I don't believe you've understood a word I've said, have you?"

"No," said Bobby simply.

"You're just a stupid little boy," she said crossly, longing to give him a good shake. "Listen!" and she started all over again. But Bobby couldn't, or wouldn't, understand. By this time Marie was beginning to recognise the fact that she was defeated. Bobby wanted a new one all right but he wanted to keep his old one as well. It was almost with relief that she heard Mrs Hobbs come in and so she quickly wiped his face and started telling him a story.

She left the house gloomily and drifted along the road, annoyed that her scheme had come to nothing. She had so looked forward to her triumph and it was particularly galling to think that she had been defeated by a stubborn little boy. She just thanked heaven that she had resisted the temptation to telephone the Major the previous evening and tell him that the puppet was as good as in his hands already. She would have looked an absolute fool, and she would have found it pretty difficult to face him after that. It was lucky really, she thought to herself, that he hadn't made getting Bobby's puppet a sort of test. But then, she reminded herself, it had never actually sounded like a matter of life or death to him. He had sounded interested, but that was about all. As he had said, it would have been a feather in his cap and in hers too, but it clearly wasn't going to be the end of everything because she hadn't succeeded. If only she had had a different child to deal with it would have been all right.

And so she wandered along, her mind so occupied that she didn't even notice that she had gone straight past Joe. He tapped her on the shoulder and she shot round in surprise. "Joe!" she cried. "I ought to have known it was you. What did you make me jump like that for?"

Joe folded his arms high on his chest and stared down at her impassively for a moment. Then slowly and deliberately he raised one arm in greeting. "How!" he growled in a deep voice.

"How what?"

"Me seek pale-face girl. Me smoke pipe of peace."

"About time too," exclaimed Marie, tossing her head in the air, "after all those lies you told my mother."

Joe looked abashed. "Me heap bad man. Me big liar. Me go tell pale-face mother," and he turned on his heels and strode away.

Marie ran after him and grabbed his sleeve. "Joe! Joe! Don't! You musn't. You know I'll get in a row. She wasn't half mad but she'd kill me if she knew what I was really up to."

Joe spun round again. He pointed to himself. "Hawk Eye good man?"

Marie nodded. "Hawk Eye good man," she agreed.

Joe whipped out an imaginary hatchet and did a war dance round her, whooping loudly, one finger in his mouth. "Pale-face maiden Hawk Eye's prisoner. We go to wigwam. Have pow-wow, make pact, drink white man's poison. Come!" He seized her by the hair and marched her along the road.

"White man's poison?" said Marie. "What's that?"

"Expresso coffee."

They entered the El Tropicana and Joe dragged her to a table behind a trough containing a number of tall plants. He put his hand to his forehead and shaded his eyes. He parted the plants carefully and cautiously peered through them. "Good," he muttered. "We haven't been spotted yet." He took a quick look all round them. "It's safe enough here . . . for the time being," he muttered in a low voice.

"Why can't we sit where I can see what's going on?" complained Marie. "I hate being shut away like this."

Joe indicated the plants. "Cover," he muttered, and took another quick furtive look through the curtain of plants. "There are a great number of people," he went on, "who

164

would be very interested in our conversation if they could manage to hear it."

Marie edged her chair a little closer to his. "Is it a secret?" she asked, consumed by curiosity.

"Sh!" Joe put his fingers to his lips. "See that girl coming over here. She's one of them."

Marie looked up. "She's only the waitress," she said.

Joe ordered coffee and cakes before he spoke again. He waited until the girl had moved away. "She's only a waitress to you," he said cryptically.

"And what's she to you?" asked Marie, a trifle jealously.

"As yet, nothing," said Joe. "I do have a shrewd suspicion, however, that she's on their side. Her real name is Fee-ling, which translated means 'O beautiful maiden from the land of orange-blossom and pagodas'."

"What's she doing with a Chinese name when she's English?"

Joe waggled his finger at her. "That's their devilish cunning," he said. "It's all done by exchanging babies. She started life in a British cradle right enough, but she was swapped for a Chinese baby one day when her mother was at the launderette. Even now her mother doesn't quite understand how her blue-eyed, golden-haired baby was changed into a slant-eyed beauty. But this one was removed to the mysterious East and brought up as a good, rice-eating, genuine Chinese girl, owing allegiance only to the Oriental world and so was sent here to steal our industrial secrets."

"What industrial secrets?"

"How to make revolting coffee like this," he said as the girl put it in front of them. "Not only how to make it, but how to get away with it as well."

Marie was furious with herself at half-believing him.

"Oh, very funny, very very funny," she said tartly. "Fancy

165

thinking you'd take me in with a feeble little story like that. I don't know why I put up with you."

"I do," said Joe. "It's my charm, my fatal charm. It's irresistible."

"Why don't you go back to your gas lamps? That's all you're good for."

Joe looked offended. "All! I'll have you know, my good girl, that the fate of Britain rests on my gas lamps. There's a prophecy about them. 'When the gas lamps go down, it's the end of London Town' — so don't go knocking my profession."

Marie snorted. "You're just a nut," she said. "I don't know why they don't lock you up. They will one day I expect."

Joe shook his head. "Were I one of the great unwashed," he said, "I dare say I should be. But we are members of the aristocracy and permitted, nay, even encouraged, in our eccentricities. It's all part of the British way of life."

"Are your family really lords and things?" asked Marie eagerly.

Joe looked horrified. "I should hope not, my little jelly-baby. We have no truck with that jumped-up crowd. No, we belong to something more ancient, more honourable."

Marie leaned forward, her chin on her hands. "Go on," she said.

Joe looked at her blankly. "Go on with what? Or should I say with what go on? No, on second thoughts perhaps I should say on with what go."

Marie stirred restlessly in her chair. "Don't be so annoying. You were saying about your family and you said you were ever so ancient."

Joe looked hurt. "Perhaps I am," he said with a sigh, "but it's hardly tactful of you to repeat it. You should have put one lovely slender arm on my shoulder and murmured that I

166

didn't look it."

Marie sat up straight again. She knew Joe well enough to know that he wasn't going to tell her any more. "Well, what have you brought me here for?" she demanded. "I bet it wasn't just for my company."

"You underrate yourself, my little acid-drop," he said. "As a matter of fact I wanted to be sure that you were still at liberty and not in hot pursuit of half the underworld of London."

"If you mean Harbottle," said Marie in a superior tone, "you can forget it. I sorted that out ages ago. As a matter of fact I got the Major to give him the push and he did. He sacked him."

"Major Graham?" asked Joe slowly. "Do you know him?"

"Why? Do you?"

Joe nodded. "Fairly friendly with him, are you?"

"Yes, he's not so bad when you get to know him," said Marie in an off-hand way, but secretly delighted at being able to speak of the Major with such familiarity. "You just have to know how to handle him."

"I see," Joe said, stirring his coffee in a thoughtful way. "I bet he didn't realise that Harbottle was really a shifty character until you raised the scales from his eyes. And what's more, I bet he's so grateful to you that he's going to reward you in some way or another."

Marie paused, fork in the air, amazed at Joe's perception. "You're not far out," she admitted. "How did you know?"

"My sweet little sugar-coated poppet, I'm really quite good at putting two and two together. You are suspicious of Harbottle and so become suspicious of the Major. You become a thundering nuisance, popping up at the most inconvenient times, and therefore the Major decides to enlist you on his side and tells you some cock and bull story that satisfies your inflated sense of importance. That's right, isn't it, Marie?" Joe looked up at Marie's face. She was red with fury but there was also a suspicion of tears in her eyes. He could have kicked himself for handling her so badly.·

She jumped to her feet and slammed down her cup. "Clever!" she shouted. "You think you know everything, don't you? Let me tell you I know exactly what I'm doing. There's no need to treat me as if . . . as if I'm Fred, because I'm not." Without thinking she shovelled more and more sugar into her cup so that it overflowed. "Since you know everything else, I suppose you know what my job is too."

"That's the one thing I don't know," Joe said quietly, "and it's probably the key to the whole thing. I was hoping you'd tell me."

Marie stirred the coffee so that drops flew in every direction. "Then you can find out for yourself," she said. "It's confidential." She suddenly pushed the coffee away and would have left, but Joe gripped her by the wrist.

"Look sweetie," he said, "you're the one I'm thinking about. I wouldn't like to see you involved in anything you couldn't handle. Now just sit down again."

Unwillingly, Marie sat down. "I can handle it," she snapped. "I don't need your help."

"The Major really is a nasty man," Joe continued as if she hadn't interrupted, "so why don't you just tell your Uncle Joe all about it?"

Marie jerked her wrist away from him and rubbed it. "You tell me what you want to know for first," she said.

Joe shook his head. "I can't." he said.

"What you mean is you won't."

"Look, there's nothing really concrete against him at the moment but the . . . various people have been watching him for some time now, and he's mixing with a very odd crowd.

The curious thing is that a lot of them seem to be ending up as guests of Her Majesty."

"What, in prison?"

"Well done, my little toasted teacake. You'll soon be top of the class."

Marie flushed. She hated it when Joe thrust down her throat that she was still at school. "Oh, that," she said, trying to regain her casual air. "He told me all about that." She rummaged around in her mind for a good lie, but it wasn't necessary. Joe was speaking again.

"You have changed your tune, haven't you?" Joe made a pattern in the spilt sugar. "The last time we had a little chat you believed in that old thing about birds of a feather."

"I know him better now."

"And I dare say you have utter and complete faith in your own judgment and none whatsoever in mine."

"It's none of your business."

"Marie," said Joe seriously, "just believe I know what I'm talking about. He's up to no good, and although I don't actually know what he's after I've got a fair idea. You really aren't old enough yet to be able to weigh people up. You still take them at their own valuation. When you're a bit more experienced . . . "

There was a crash as Marie jumped up and knocked over her cup. She rushed out of the place and into the street, trying to keep back the tears that sprang to her eyes.

Joe jumped to his feet too and started to go after her. The waitress barred his path. "Where's your bill?" she said indignantly and gave him a suspicious look. "I gave you one."

"I know," he said absently, staring at the door. He pulled out ten shillings. "I know. Be a good girl and pay it for me."

"It's not my job," she said resentfully.

"That's my girl," he said, squeezing past her and dashing

into the street. He was too late. Marie was out of sight. There wasn't much point, he thought, in dashing madly round and round in an aimless way. He was sure to see her sooner or later and would be able to put it right.

Marie had fought back her tears by this time and was wandering back in the direction of her home. Although she kept reminding herself of the success she had scored with the Major, Joe had somehow made her feel terribly depressed, so she was delighted when she banged into Bernie.

"Marie!" he cried, patting her on the head. "You can't imagine what a dreary Saturday I had. All that dreadful rain and not even a glimpse of you to brighten things up. I kept thinking that if you'd only pop up the sky would clear and the sun would shine. Now you musn't neglect me like that. No Marie, no customers, that's what it's beginning to look like. I really ought to pay you a retainer to be my mascot."

Marie flashed him one of her brightest smiles and went on beaming. It was nice to know she still had one fan.

CHAPTER TEN

The following day was the dress rehearsal, and not only did the cast rush around in a frenzied way but so did most of the school. In spite of the head's pious hope that the routine wouldn't be too interrupted, it was quite impossible for anyone to be unaffected. There was tremendous activity in the hall. The art master and some of the sixth form had designed the set, which had been made in the workshop. There was incessant tapping and hammering as it was erected on the stage. Some of the costumes had been made in the needlework class and these were being tried on and altered for the very last time. Mr May was having a session in the playground with the soldiers and his explosive cries of "Left foot forward, Fred, left foot! No, not that one, your *left* foot!" could be heard all over the school.

Since so many of the staff were helping with the last minutes preparations some teachers had to take more than one class at a time and many children were squeezed in together. Marie was in a class taken by Miss Tolly, who looked very apprehensive at the mob facing her.

It wasn't long before paper darts were flying around. One caught Marie on the nose and she picked up her rubber and hurled it back in the same direction. One of the boys picked it up and threw it at a girl who was bent over a piece of paper. She looked up. "Who threw that?" she demanded indignantly.

Miss Tolly turned round from the blackboard. "Who threw what?"

Pat held up the rubber. "This," she said crossly. "It smudged my drawing."

"What drawing? You're not supposed to be drawing. Come on now, what drawing?"

"I was trying to draw a picture of the Squeeze Box," said Pat reluctantly.

"The Squeeze Box?" Miss Tolly looked puzzled. "What Squeeze Box?"

For a moment or two there was a shocked silence in the room as the class looked at each other, incredulity on their faces, and then there was sudden uproar as they all burst out at once.

"You *must* know."

"You're joking!"

"They're at number one."

"She's kidding. She must be."

"There isn't another group . . . "

" . . . the newest sound."

"You must know their new one," shouted one of the boys above the hubbub. "It goes like this 'A-one, a-two, a-three, aback, away, around . . .'." Within seconds the whole class was singing, beating out the rhythm with their feet, pounding on their desks and rocking in their seats.

Miss Tolly, appalled at the noise, stood there, her back against the blackboard, far too inexperienced to deal with the whole hideous situation. Quite suddenly the door of the classroom was flung open with a crash that reverberated throughout the school and there, framed in the doorway, quivering with rage, was Mr Marsh. The noise ceased like magic except for the quavering voice of Pat, who was still swaying to and fro, her eyes closed. "I wanna die, I wanna die," she wailed. There were a few nervous giggles as the last words died away and Pat, suddenly conscious of her solo performance, opened her eyes and sat frozen, open-mouthed as Mr Marsh towered over her.

There was total silence as he looked at them all in utter disgust. They all stared back, hardly breathing, almost sick with hideous anticipation. "I am so angry," he said, "that I dare not punish you at this moment." There was an almost audible sigh of relief and the slightest air of almost imperceptible relaxation. "Do not imagine that this is something that can simply be forgotten and forgiven. You have all of you behaved abominably, and your conduct has been more disgraceful than anything I have ever witnessed before. And what is worse, it has happened in front of a visitor to this school."

It wouldn't have taken place in front of anyone else, thought Marie to herself, none of them would have been daft enough to try it on the staff. Her face, however, registered the same ashamed expression as everybody else. "And so," concluded Mr Marsh, giving them one last contemptuous look, "I shall see you all here at four o'clock, when I shall get to the bottom of this insane outbreak." He withdrew as suddenly as he had arrived. Miss Tolly, who had by now pulled herself together, began the lesson in a silence that was so complete that one really could have heard the proverbial pin drop.

For the rest of the day there wasn't a better behaved or more cooperative class in the school, although Marie felt that they might just have well gone on to have a jolly good time, since they were all heading straight for the tumbrils anyway.

Meanwhile, Miss Fisher had a last inspection of the cast in their costumes. At least it would be the best-dressed play she had ever put on, and secretly she thought it might be the most successful one too. A slight frown passed across her forehead as she looked at Fred, who was either not quite in his clothes or was somehow just coming out of them. There seemed an extraordinary gap between the top half of his garments and the bottom. She took a quick look at the rest of the soldiers. They were all right. She was just about to tell him to pull his jacket down and his trousers up and then she glanced at his placid face and changed her mind. It would be just like him, she thought, to pull so hard that either the top fell to pieces or the bottom got split. No, much better to leave him alone while he was still calm and confident. She turned to Maggie instead. "You really do look most attractive, Maggie. That dress does suit you, doesn't it? Are you going to put your hair up?"

"Yes, Miss Fisher," said Maggie. "Mum's going to do it for me."

"And did you manage to find something nice to put in your hair? Something shiny or sparkly would be best."

"Well," Maggie looked doubtful. "Mum did have some beads, but I broke them. But she promised to get me some more. She won't forget, I'm sure she won't. Not when she's promised."

"I'll tell you what," said Miss Fisher. "I'll bring something just in case there's a mishap, and then you won't have anything to worry about."

"Super," cried Maggie. "Thanks, Miss Fisher."

Miss Fisher turned round to the rest of the cast. "Right," she said briskly. "Now we will have a straight run through so you'll get used to the scenery. All those in the first scene on stage, please." She inspected them carefully "Good. The King and the Queen on stage. Leo, sit down on your chair. Everyone else in the wings." She looked at those who were not in the scene. "Now you sit quietly. I don't want a peep out of any of you."

Right from the beginning the rehearsal went so well that she could hardly believe it. It seemed too good to be true. Fred marched in the wrong direction once but that was the only mishap. The girls managed their long skirts beautifully and everyone's voice was audible. The music had been well-chosen and Maggie sang her song without a trace of the nervousness Miss Fisher knew she must be feeling. After the first part she called a halt. "You really deserve a break," she said. "Apart from one or two little things I will mention when it's all over, it has run very smoothly indeed. If you keep this up you will find yourselves going home earlier for a change. Now don't disturb the rest of the school, but go into the cloakrooms or the playground — or stay here if you'd rather — but I shall want you back in exactly twenty minutes." She hurried towards the door but turned back, smiling. "By the way, that box on the piano is full of chocolate biscuits. I thought you might be hungry. It was terribly heavy to bring so I don't want to have to take it home again. I'd far rather you emptied it so that it can be thrown away," and she walked off.

There was a stunned silence for a moment. "Crikey!" said Leo, making for the piano. "She doesn't seem like a teacher, does she? She sounds human!"

The dress rehearsal was over by three and Miss Fisher informed the jubilant cast that the head had given permission for them all to go home early. So, under the envious eyes of the rest of the school, they crept into their classrooms to collect their bags before rushing out into the street.

Marie glowered as she watched Maggie leave. It was just

175

about the last straw as far as she was concerned. "She's going early because she can sing," she said to herself, "and we're going late because we can't." However, she bent over her book again and tried to look as if she really cared about the life of the tadpole in an effort to avoid yet more trouble.

At four o'clock the bell went, and almost before the first clangings had died away there was the tramping of feet and the raised voices of those who were fortunate enough to go home. Slowly the bangings and slammings died away and there was silence throughout the school while Marie's form worked on. They bent even more diligently over their books. There was hardly a sound in the room except for the rustling of pages and the occasional scratching of pens, or the sudden self-conscious cough that made them look up. Surely all this industry must make some impression, they thought. The time dragged on and still no one moved or spoke, and then they heard the heavy and deliberate footsteps of Mr Marsh approaching. They looked up as he entered the room. "Now," he said ominously, "let us have our little talk!"

Joe was waiting outside the school as they all came out. He half expected Marie to be first; it wasn't like her to drag her heels at home time. Finally he stopped one of the stragglers and asked. "Oh, her," said the boy. "She must have gone early with Alan and that lot."

Joe hovered indecisively on the pavement for a moment or two. He really did want to see her. His best chance, he thought at last, was to go to Maggie's. So he walked round and, since the door was wide open, went straight in.

Alan, Maggie, Leo and Fred were all munching their way through great chunks of toast and drinking tea. "Do you want some, Joe?" asked Maggie, delighted to see him. "I'll stick a slice under the grill for you." She poured him out a cup of tea and pushed him into the most comfortable chair

176

"Lovely," said Joe, stretching out his long legs. "Don't spare the butter, Maggie. I shall soon be taking up my new job with the National Union of Dairy Cows and I must get into condition. I've got to eat a ton of butter every fifteen days to prove my heart's in the right place."

"Why every fifteen days?" asked Fred.

"Because, my dear Fred, it's one day longer than a fortnight."

"Oh," mumbled Fred, as he crammed his mouth full. "I see."

Joe put his cup down and dragged his chair a bit nearer the table. "As a matter of fact," he said confidentially, "I haven't decided to take the job. I'm really considering various offers before I make up my mind."

"What offers?" asked Leo, wiping a dribble of butter from his chin.

"Well, there's managing a treacle factory, though that could get a bit sticky, and there's being a big wheel in a bicycle factory or . . . "

"But what about the gas lamps?" asked Fred. "You keep saying they musn't go out."

"And neither must they," said Joe quickly. "That would be utter disaster. But I think I'll have time to keep them going. It's only a part-time job really. By the way, do you know where Marie is? I've been looking for her for some time."

"Yes," said Maggie promptly. "She's got to go over and spend the night with her Granny. Her Mum said she'd got to."

"Now that," murmured Joe, "is a very great pity."

"Is it?" said Alan.

"Yes, I rather wanted to squeeze her squalid little secret out of her tonight. You don't know where her Granny lives?" They all shook their heads. "Oh, well," he said, getting up,

177

"never mind. If she's with her grandmother she can't get into much mischief between tonight and tomorrow. I'm sure to see her at the play, aren't I? I'll keep an eye open for her there."

Maggie jumped to her feet. "Are you coming then?" she asked delightedly.

"I wouldn't miss it for anything," said Joe warmly. "I might be just a little bit late though. I've got a few ends to tidy up first, but with any luck I shall manage to see most of it. Feeling nervous, are you? Exotic butterflies in churning tummy and all that?"

"I expect I should have," said Maggie, "but I don't."

"Quite right," declared Joe. "It's only the bad actresses who feel nervous and go round boring everyone about it. The really good ones usually get a sick feeling just before they go on. You'll see, Doctor Joe the actor's medico will be proved right once again. Just before you go on you'll find your stomach turning over and you'll feel as sick as a dog and you'll think you've forgotten your lines. That's the best sign of all. Feel that and you'll give a fabulous performance. Normally, when I'm in Harley Street, that bit of advice costs fifteen guineas, you know. But for you, my dear Sarah, it's free." He gave her a quick wave and strode out of the room.

"Isn't Joe super?" said Maggie, standing at the window and watching him run down the steps. "He's got a way of making me feel I'm somebody and not just anybody."

"Me too," said Fred. "Got any more tea?"

"No," said Alan firmly. "Stop eating and go and help with the washing up. Maggie's mum will be back soon and we want to get the place tidied up."

Alan and Leo cleared the table and Maggie handed Fred a tea-towel. "It's your turn to dry," she said as she turned on the water. "Try to be careful though. Mum hasn't got over hose two chipped plates and the broken cup yet."

Leo snatched the tea-towel away from Fred's unresisting hands. "I'll do it for you," he said. "You help Alan straighten up."

They were just finishing as Mrs Hobbs came in and they rushed to take the heavy shopping bags from her. "I'll make you some tea, Mum," Maggie said, seeing how tired she looked.

Mrs Hobbs shook her head. "No thanks, lovey," she said. "I only popped in to get rid of this load and to leave Bobby with you. I've got to go out again, but I'll be back as quick as I can."

"Another job?" asked Alan sympathetically as she went out again.

"Yes," sighed Maggie. "I wish I could help. It's not fair. Mum has to go out cleaning at all hours and she's always tired."

Alan looked at the shopping. "Well, at least we can put this lot away," he said. "You keep an eye on Bobby, Fred. He likes you best."

Fred beamed with delight. "What shall we play with?" he asked.

Bobby, who had been sitting quietly in the corner looking at his battered old cars, looked up hopefully at him but said nothing.

"What do you want?" asked Maggie. Bobby didn't bother to answer her but he shifted his gaze to Leo.

"I know," said Leo suddenly. "We told him not to cart his old puppet around with him." He turned to Bobby. "It's all right," he said. "You can play with it while we're here."

"What made you say that?" asked Maggie, as Bobby disappeared upstairs. "I wondered why he'd given up taking it to school."

"I didn't mean not to play with it here," explained Le[d] awkwardly. "I just meant he shouldn't take it outside. Yo[u] see it could be worth something, and Fred and me thought o[f] taking it to Bernie to find out. I thought it would be a pity i[f] he lost it or something before we knew. After all, that ma[n] was keen enough to want to buy it, and if we knew what w[e] could get for it — if ever Bobby felt like giving it up — the[n] we'd know what we could ask for it." He finished his speec[h] in a state of confusion.

"I ought to have thought of that," said Alan enthusias[-] tically. "Bobby might have dropped it or lost it any old time[,] and it just could be worth something. Let's take it along t[o] Bernie like you said. We'll have to find time to go tomorrow[.]

At this moment Bobby trotted back into the roo[m] clutching his puppet. He took it straight over to Fred an[d] held it out to him. "Dance!" he said.

Fred obligingly picked the puppet up and jigged it aroun[d] and waved its legs about wildly. Then he frowned an[d] stopped and looked at it carefully. "What have you don[e] with it, Bobby? It's got ever so thin."

"Puppet must dance!" said Bobby sternly.

Fred turned it upside down. "You've been starving i[t] haven't you, Bobby?" Bobby giggled and shook his hea[d.] "Well, it's lost some weight somehow. Look at it, Alan."

Alan glanced up. "It looks just the same to me, Fred."

"Well, it's not," said Fred. Bobby tugged at his sleev[e] again, looking very impatient, so he concentrated on makin[g] it perform a wild dance all over the floor until it collapsed.

"More!" cried Bobby. "Make it a clown."

Fred obediently made it stand on one leg and fall over, an[d] balance on its nose and fall over, and then he made it try t[o] jump over a book. Bobby lay on the floor chuckling. Finall[y] he made it turn a series of cartwheels, so that it ended upsid[e] down with its frock over its head. Fred looked at it more closely. "Hey! Look at this," he shouted. "It's got a socking great hole in its tummy. I can put three of my fingers in it."

"I expect it's always been there," said Maggie, sorting out the knives and forks.

"I didn't see it before," said Fred. "It must have lost some of its stuffing. I said it felt lighter, didn't I?" He glanced down at Bobby, who was tugging away at his sweater. "All right, Bobby. There's no need to pull me to pieces. My Mum'll be after your blood if you make a hole. You just watch. I'm going to make it walk the tight-rope." Actually Fred was finding the hole very useful indeed. By sticking his fingers in it he was able to jerk the arms in a much more realistic way. Slowly he made the puppet walk closer and closer to Bobby, the arms swaying about from side to side, and then suddenly the arms swung forward and tweaked Bobby's nose. Bobby screamed with laughter and rolled over and over on to the floor screaming "More! More!"

"That's quite enough," said Maggie firmly, as she hung up the tea-towel. "You won't be able to go to sleep properly if you get so excited, and then Mum'll be cross with you. It's no good looking at Fred like that either. It's all over for tonight."

Alan and Leo got to their feet. "We'd better be going, Maggie," said Alan. "What are you doing tomorrow?"

"Don't know," said Maggie. "Same as any Saturday, I suppose. The shopping will still have to be done and Bobby will have to be looked after."

"We'll call for you then," said Alan. "Why don't we all go up to Bernie's then? He's never really busy in the mornings."

"Fine," shouted Maggie, standing at the top of the steps to see them go. "Bet you Bernie thinks we're round the bend when he sees what we've come for." Standing on tiptoe to give them a last wave she saw her mother, now looking very tired indeed, come round the corner and she darted inside to put the kettle on. "I'll have the tea ready in a moment," she shouted as she heard her mother come in. "You don't half look whacked."

"Thanks." Her mother sank down and eased off her shoes. "It's been a long day." She fumbled under the chair and found her old slipppers and put them on. "How was the rehearsal then?"

"Smashing!" said Maggie emphatically, as she swilled hot water round the inside of the teapot. "The scenery's marvellous. It almost looks real and you wouldn't recognise most of them with their make-up on. Miss Fisher let us go early because she was so pleased."

Her mother rested her arms on the sides of the chair. "It's lovely just to sit down," she said. "What time have you got to be at school tomorrow, Maggie?"

"It's starting at three, but all the main ones have got to be there by half past one and the others have got to get there at two," Maggie said, pouring the hot water into the pot. "Mum, you will be able to come, won't you?"

Her mother laughed. "I'd be a funny sort of mother if I didn't. Your brothers are going to try and get over as well, but it'll be a bit difficult because they're both working in the morning."

Maggie looked up in astonishment. "Really? Fancy them coming all that way."

"You'd be surprised if you knew how many people are coming. As far as I can make out they might as well close the market down for the day."

Maggie looked horrified. "They can't," she said. "I might not be good enough."

"I'm only pulling your leg, Maggie, but a number of people

did say they'd try to pop in for a bit of it. And you really don't have to worry. If you're good enough for Miss Fisher then you're good enough for everyone else," said her mother firmly. "This is a good cup of tea, Maggie. It's just what I wanted. Anyway, even if you do forget your words, it won't really matter, not if you look as nice as you did the other night."

Maggie was absolutely overwhelmed at this praise from her mother. "Oh, I don't know," she said. "Marie's prettier."

"Marie's pretty enough, all right," agreed her mother. "The only trouble with her is that she never forgets it. Ever since she was a tiny little thing her mother has told her that she's prettier and cleverer and better than anybody else and so she puts on those airs and gets herself thoroughly disliked."

"She's not always like that," protested Maggie. "You know she's not. She's changed a lot lately."

"And not before time," said her mother.

Maggie was anxious to change the subject. "Mum," she said, "did you manage to get the beads for my hair?"

Her mother nodded. "I saw some pretty red ones on a stall this morning and I thought how nice they'd look in your dark hair and so I bought them. As a matter of fact I bought some wide bracelets that go with them as well. I just couldn't resist them."

Maggie hopped up. "Can I look?" she asked eagerly.

"Not just now, Maggie. I put them in a drawer out of Bobby's reach. I'll get them later on when there's a bit more time. I want to give Bobby something to eat and get him upstairs to bed. I'll get on with the cooking and you lay the table for me."

Somehow there was such a lot to do that evening it was past nine o'clock before Maggie and her mother stopped work. They looked round the tidy kitchen with the newly-ironed clothes airing on the clothes-horse and the pile of mending. "That's a good evening's work," said Mrs Hobbs in a satisfied tone. "Now up you go, Maggie, and get straight into bed. This is one time you really need a good night's rest. You can read for a bit if you want. I've got to go out early tomorrow, so I'll leave a shopping list on the table. I'll be back in plenty of time to get you something to eat and off to school, so there's no need to worry about that. Now, up you go and I'll pop in and switch the light out."

It wasn't until Maggie was in bed that she realised that she really was tired, and although she immediately began reciting her lines to herself, somehow her eyes just closed and she fell fast asleep.

CHAPTER ELEVEN

The following morning Maggie woke very early and lay in bed for a few minutes wondering what it would actually be like to walk on the stage with a real audience in front of her. She tried to imagine it, but somehow the whole thing seemed so unreal that she soon gave up. I'll find out soon enough, she thought, as she clambered out of bed and washed and cleaned her teeth. There was a note on the kitchen table together with a shopping list, some money and a bottle of shampoo. "Wash your hair and see it's really clean and don't forget your neck," it read. Maggie smiled to herself. Whenever anything out of the ordinary was happening her mother left a note about washing her neck. "Suppose you had an accident," her mother would say, "whatever would people say if you had a dirty neck?" And Maggie knew by now that it was no good pointing out that if she had an accident no one would care. If she did say anything her mother simply came and scrubbed her neck for her.

Once Maggie was dressed she woke Bobby and washed and dressed him and they both had breakfast and then hurried out to do the shopping. Since it was early and there were few people around they managed to get everything done in record time. She was amazed to find how many of the stall-holders wished her luck. The old lady on the corner who sold flowers stopped Maggie on her way home and gave her a large bunch of them and said she was going to try to sell out early so that she could pop into the performance. For the first time Maggie began to feel that she really was the star.

They had just got home and she was putting the flowers in water when there was a loud hammering on the door and Bobby ran and opened it. She could hear him talking to the boys so she shouted, "I'm just going to wash my hair. I won't be half a minute."

"That means about half an hour," said Alan with a sigh, plonking himself down on a chair.

"It only takes me about a minute," said Fred.

"I can see that," said Leo. "It sticks out a mile."

"Does it?" Fred looked anxious. "I couldn't find a comb," he said. "I had to part it with a pencil."

Maggie came back, rubbing her hair briskly. "Here you are," she said. "Use Bobby's. He won't mind." She shook her hair out and brushed it rapidly. "I'm ready now," she said.

"You can't go out with dripping wet hair like that," said Leo, a scandalized look on his face. "It's soaking."

"You'll catch a cold, and then you won't be able to sing," said Fred warningly.

"Colds take three days to come out. Everyone knows that and I shan't mind if I have to stay off school next week. I won't half seem dull, just doing lessons and getting put in detention." She sighed heavily and attacked her hair with the brush again. Then she threw it down. "There. I've done," she said.

Alan put his hand on the top of her head and then ostentatiously dried it on his handkerchief. "You must be potty, Maggie. Let's stay here for a bit and give it a chance to dry. We could go through your part while we're waiting."

"No thank you!" said Maggie emphatically. "I might find I'd forgotten it. Look, the sun's shining and I'll bet you anything you like that it'll be dry in ten minutes. Come on!"

Bobby was already holding his puppet and he ran to the door as she spoke, so she bundled the boys out after him and banged the door behind her. The three boys trailed after her feeling that she really ought not to be out with wet hair but not knowing quite what to do about it, while Bobby ran ahead, stopping every now and again to make his puppet walk on a wall or dance round a lamp-post.

The streets were crowded by now with the usual Saturday shoppers, but they threaded their way through and finally managed to reach Bernie's. "It's gone!" Maggie exclaimed, stopping so suddenly that Fred crashed into her.

"What has? What's gone?" he asked.

"Bernie's great big fire-place," said Leo. "I didn't think he'd ever get rid of it."

"Your lack of faith amazes me," said Bernie, squeezing past the furniture and trying to struggle into his jacket at the same time. "I know we all thought what an utterly revolting piece it was, but then you must remember that the world is full of utterly revolting people and sometimes we manage to match them up." He gave up the struggle to come out and beckoned them in instead. "Come along and I'll show you some really dreadful china. It's quite frightful, but it will go like hot cakes, you mark my words."

"We really came to ask your advice, Bernie," said Alan as they all filtered in. "Do you know anything about puppets?"

Bernie ran his fingers through his fringe of hair. "Not really," he admitted, "though I must confess it goes against the grain to admit it. The last time I had anything to do with puppets was when I went to a beastly little exhibition. It was absolutely crammed with the strangest people, all hand-woven

187

tweeds and sandals. You know the type. It quite put me off."

"But could you tell if one was old or valuable?"

"Oh, I should think I could just about manage that. Fred, dear boy, do stop wriggling. You'll knock that awful lamp over if you don't watch out, and then where should we be? You can keep still too, Bobby, but first of all just go and throw that nauseating bundle of old rags in the gutter before you contaminate us all."

"But that's it, Bernie," said Leo hastily, seeing Bobby's face puckering up. He was ready to burst into tears at the least thing. "That's the one we want to know about. Give it to me, Bobby, so Bernie can have a closer look." Bobby started to conceal it under his jumper. "Now don't be silly," he said sharply. "You can have it back again."

"Just hold it up at a distance, Bobby," said Bernie hastily, shuddering at the thought of handling it. "I can get a much better idea from further off. That's right, not too close. Now turn it over for me and tip it upside down." They all stared anxiously at Bernie's face. "Now put it straight again," he said and looked hard, his head on one side.

"What do you think?" asked Leo excitedly.

"I think you should throw it straight into an incinerator," said Bernie instantly. "It's probably covered with the most loathsome and evil germs."

"Isn't it valuable?" asked Fred, disappointed.

"Of course not," said Bernie briskly. "Strictly speaking, it's not a puppet at all. Whatever made you think it was?"

"Somebody offered Bobby quite a lot of money for it," explained Alan. "He told Leo and Fred that it was a collector's piece."

"The only collector who might conceivably be interested in that vile piece of garbage would be the driver of the municipal dustcart and he might well demand danger money," said Bernie, shuddering slightly as he peered at it once more. "I'm afraid that your collector friend must have been totally insane. It's nothing but a tatty old toy." Having given his verdict he reached behind him and produced a teapot. "Now just look at this," he said, waving it around. "Observe the thickness of it, note the shape, a truly hideous shape, I think you'll agree, and look at those violent colours. Now this little thing will find a new home in no time at all." He stroked it rather proudly. "You'll have to go a long way to find anything quite as vile as this."

"But do you think the puppet . . . " began Leo.

Bernie put the teapot down rather crossly. "It's really no good going on about it, Leo," he said. "No one in his right mind would give you tuppence for it. I can only repeat that anyone who offered you anything must either have been out of his mind or a poseur, though what good it would do anyone to be a poseur of puppets, I really can't imagine."

"He didn't look daft," muttered Leo.

Bernie dragged his duster out from his coat pocket and began wiping the teapot lid. "And where's your charming little friend? You're usually all together on Saturdays."

"She went to her Granny last night," said Maggie, "but she's sure to be here later."

Bernie beamed. "Now isn't that just like her? I do feel it's so typical of her to give up one of her valuable evenings just to brighten up the life of an old lady." They all nudged each other at that. "Ah, well, dear friends, I feel it's most uncivil of me to ask you to move on, but I have a feeling the public will come stampeding along at any moment and I really must concentrate on making a grubby shilling or two this morning, since I shall close this afternoon."

"Close!" Alan was amazed. "You never close on Saturdays."

Bernie stabbed a podgy finger at Maggie. "It's all her

189

fault," he said. "She's to blame. I never miss a debut, you know. You'll just have to make it worth my while, Maggie, so that when I'm starving in the gutter I shall at least have a beautiful memory to feast on."

Maggie blushed and edged out of the shop in an embarrassed way. After a brief struggle with a drawer handle Bernie followed them out and waved his duster at them as they drifted back down the street.

Leo felt terribly disappointed. Secretly he'd managed to convince himself that the puppet was worth a fortune and now that his hopes were completely dashed he felt depressed. The others, although they had never been as hopeful as Leo, were feeling slightly gloomy too. Only Bobby was happy, and he skipped down the road in a carefree way. He hadn't understood everything that was going on, but at least he realised his puppet was safe at last.

"I didn't know what Bernie meant about that man," mumbled Fred.

"You wouldn't," snapped Leo. He couldn't be bothered to explain.

"But what was he getting at?" persisted Fred. "About him being a posy or whatever it was."

"It's about time you learnt your own language," commented Leo sourly. "Anyone would think you'd come straight out of a tree to hear you speak."

Maggie slid her arm through Fred's. "All that about being a poseur?" she asked. "It was a new one for me too. I expect it meant pretending to be someone you aren't."

Fred's face cleared. "Like Joe," he said. "Anyway, it's what I keep on saying. He just wanted to get hold of the puppet and he didn't care how he did it."

Alan turned round and laughed. "A lot of good it would do him! What would he want with an old puppet with half its stuffing gone? No, I think Bernie was much nearer the mark when he said he must be bonkers."

"But they didn't think he looked bonkers," said Maggie thoughtfully.

Alan suddenly pointed to a clock. "Look at the time," he said. "You'll have to zoom, Maggie, or you won't get anything to eat."

"Gosh! I didn't know it was so late." She caught hold of Bobby's hand. "Come on, we'll have to run all the way."

They dived into the mass of shoppers and weaved their way in and out of the stalls. They wriggled through queues and darted through the large groups of people who were doing nothing but standing around staring, and finally arrived, panting and dishevelled, just as Mrs Hobbs was dishing up their lunch.

"Fancy coming in so late," she said disapprovingly as she glanced at Maggie's flushed face. "You'll make yourself sick dashing around like that. Now sit down quietly and eat up your dinner."

"Must I, Mum? I don't really feel like it. Can't I just have a cup of tea?"

"No, you can't, Maggie. You'll come over all faint on the stage if you've got an empty stomach." She noticed how apprehensively Maggie was eyeing her plate. "Just eat a little," she said persuasively. "Bobby! Just put that chip back on your plate. Use your fork. Don't let me see you picking things up in your fingers again."

Although Maggie didn't really feel like eating anything at all, she pecked at everything just to please her mother. Although her mother appeared to be busy in the kitchen she kept a sharp eye on Maggie, well aware of how nervous she was. "That'll do," she said at last. "Leave it if you don't want any more. Now go and have a good wash and then I'll do your hair."

191

Maggie looked at the clock. "I'll be late," she said wildly. "I've got to go. Miss Fisher will think I'm not coming."

Her mother took her by the shoulders and propelled her in the direction of the sink. "Nonsense," she said firmly. "You can't go without a wash and you'll feel a lot better when you've had one. And don't forget to scrub that neck while you're about it." Much to her surprise Maggie did feel a lot better after a wash, and she went back to her mother who was waiting with the brush, comb and hairpins ready. "Come along," she said, "and sit here." She gave Maggie's neck a quick scrutiny and then began brushing the long dark hair.

"Can you be quick?" asked Maggie, twisting her neck to look anxiously at the time.

Her mother pushed her head to the front again. "More haste less speed," she said and continued brushing.

Maggie tried hard to keep still but her impatience got the better of her at last. "Please!" she cried in an agonised voice. "It's ever so late."

Her mother sighed. "Actually, Maggie," she said, "I'm pretty good at telling the time myself. I'm being as quick as I can, but you don't make it any easier for me squirming around like that." However, she put down the brush and comb, and taking hold of the mass of hair, she swept it up and fixed it into place. "There," she said, "how does that look?"

Maggie leapt up and stared anxiously in the mirror. "It's lovely, Mum. You ought to have been a hairdresser. But I'd better go or else Miss Fisher . . . " The rest of her sentence was lost as she dashed out of the house.

Mrs Hobbs and Bobby left together about half an hour later and Fred, seeing them ahead of him, thundered after them. "Hallo, Mrs Hobbs, hallo, Bobby. I'm glad you've got your puppet. I bet he'll like the play," he said, as Bobby waggled the puppet under his nose.

"What do you think it's going to be like, Fred?" Mrs Hobbs asked.

"Smashing!" said Fred simply. "It'll be smashing!"

"Maggie said the costumes were lovely."

"Mine is," said Fred proudly. "Maggie's isn't bad. I think she'd have looked better in a crown than things in her hair though."

Mrs Hobbs put her hand to her mouth. "Oh, Fred!" she said. "What a good thing you came along. I'd completely forgotten the beads and the bracelets. Do you think you could go back and get them for me? Your legs are a lot younger than mine. Here's the key. You'll find them upstairs in the big bedroom in the top drawer of that old chest. Pop them in a bag and take them along with you, will you?"

"All right then," said Fred, only too pleased to help. "I'll have to get a move on though, I mustn't be late for the make-up. Miss Fisher says I've got a difficult face." He turned round and lumbered off.

By this time Maggie had already reached the school gates and she was standing there trying to get her breath back when she saw Marie approaching. "Have a good time?" she asked.

"With my granny? Are you kidding?"

"Joe was round last night looking for you," Maggie remarked.

"Oh, was he?" Marie sounded uninterested. "Pity! I'm going to be fairly busy from now on. I don't suppose I'll be able to spare the time to see him much."

Maggie suddenly noticed that Marie was looking even smarter than usual in a new white skirt and navy sweater, and she was wearing new navy shoes too. "Gosh! You look smashing!" she said admiringly. "I wish I'd got something new too. I'm sick of my uniform. Still, you're sure to meet

Joe this afternoon. He said he was going to come to the play."

Marie suddenly looked uncomfortable and clicked the catch of her shoulder bag backwards and forwards. "I . . . I, well, I'm not going to be there, Maggie," she said awkwardly. "I've got a date in Kensington, honest I have. I was coming but this . . . "

"You're not coming!" Maggie could hardly believe it. "It won't be the same if you're not there. We've always done things together. I've never let you down when you were in things and I wasn't, you know I haven't."

"Well, you know how it is," said Marie, twirling her bag round and round, "that was when we were kids, wasn't it?" Actually she was feeling a bit guilty at running out on Maggie and in her attempt to hide it she just sounded terribly superior. "I mean, things change, don't they? At least they do for me."

"Do they?" muttered Maggie miserably.

Marie edged away. "Sorry, Maggie. Honestly I'm sorry." She hovered uncertainly, while Maggie just stood there looking utterly depressed. "Oh, well," she said awkwardly. "I mustn't be late for my date." It wasn't until she had gone some yards that she remembered to turn round and wish Maggie luck, but it was too late. Maggie had gone.

She herself felt pretty miserable as she went down the Portobello Road. She hadn't wanted to make Maggie unhappy and it was true that Maggie had always supported her whatever she'd done, in spite of their frequent rows. However, once she'd got on to the bus and was on her way to Kensington she tried to shrug it off with the thought that Maggie would soon be so busy that she'd forget all about her absence. She began to think instead about her coming triumph over Joe when he found out what she'd really been doing. It would be best, she thought, to let it drop casually and then let him know just how much specialised knowledge she'd picked up. "The Major and I," she was saying rather grandly to herself when the conductor touched her on the arm. "I thought you said Kensington," he said, and she had to grab her bag and leap off quickly.

The High Street was busy enough. There were crowds of people around and for a moment Marie felt anxious at the thought that she might miss him. However, they kept on moving past and Marie, looking up at the clock, saw that she had over a quarter of an hour to wait. First of all she went down the arcade that led to the tube station, just to make sure that Major Graham wasn't waiting there. Then she sauntered back towards the street, examining and criticising everything that caught her eye in the shop windows. The clothes she saw she thought were hopelessly out of date and only fit for fat old ladies. Perhaps, she thought, only fat old ladies shopped here. She looked enviously across the road to where hordes of thin and trendy girls were rushing up and down the road. She was longing to go across the road and look in the shops they went into, but it was nearly three o'clock by now and she didn't want to risk missing him. She took a last quick look at her reflection in a shop window, arranged the fall of hair so that it covered one shoulder and wondered for the hundredth time whether she could ever get out of the house wearing eye make-up without being spotted. Well, maybe her mother would stop treating her like a kid once she was able to flaunt her job in her face.

By this time it was past three, so she wandered back to the tube station and examined the people who were hanging round. There was no doubt about it, the Major was late. She walked restlessly from the station to the street and back from the street to the station. The crowds were still milling

around, but she was positive that she hadn't missed him
Glumly she leaned against a shop window where she had a
reasonably good view in both directions and settled down
After twenty minutes of waiting her original good-humour
had fled and so had her depression. What she now felt was
straightforward fury. He had stopped her from going to see
Maggie, she decided. He had made her quarrel with her
friends, he had forced her to drag down to Kensington just to
see some piddling little exhibition and, the most heinous
crime of all, he had left her hanging around on her own. She
would have plenty to say to him when he eventually arrived

She drifted back to the entrance to the station and hung
around there gloomily for several minutes, forced, out of
sheer boredom, to read the posters advertising concerts and
films. Suddenly she spotted one for Holland House. That was
where Major Graham had said they were going. She moved
closer to read it. There was a concert and an exhibition of
painting and sculpture. That was all. There was nothing about
dolls. That's strange, she thought. She went straight over to
the ticket collector. "Is there anything else on at Holland
Park?" she asked, tapping him on the back.

He jerked his head at the poster. "Can't you read?"

"All right," said Marie. "I only asked."

"What do you think they put posters up for?" he said in a
surly tone. "If there was anything different it'd say so
wouldn't it?"

Marie stared rudely at his bald head. "Keep your hair on,"
she said coldly as she walked away and back to the High
Street. She nibbled at her thumb-nail thoughtfully. She knew
it was the right time and the right place, and the Major wasn't
the sort of person to forget about it. He might have had an
accident, of course, but since there wasn't any exhibition
anyway, it looked as if he had got her down there

196

deliberately for reasons of his own. It looked as if he had taken her for a fool. The thought of it made her so angry that on the spur of the moment she decided to dash across the road and catch the bus she could see waiting at the traffic lights. She looked neither to right nor left, but plunged abruptly into the traffic and started to run across. There was the sudden roar of an engine and Marie, looking up, saw a car practically on top of her. There was a screech as it swerved in her direction just as she launched herself at the kerb and she scrambled to safety while the car, without slackening speed, accelerated away. Hands reached out and helped Marie up. "You silly, silly girl," cried a woman, nearly as white-faced and shaken as Marie herself. "You nearly got yourself killed. I don't know how he missed you. He's had to stop at the lights and I wouldn't blame him if he came back and gave you a piece of his mind."

Marie, still trembling, stood there brushing herself down and gazed absently at the car. Suddenly she shook off the woman's hand. The car seemed remarkably familiar to her. She was sure she had seen it before. As the lights turned green and the traffic began to move round the corner, the driver half-turned in his seat. It was the Major! Now she knew where she had seen it before. It had been in the Portobello when she was with Alan. Mindless of her bruises, she bolted up the road after it, but as she did so it glided away and was out of sight long before she reached it. Frustrated, muttering to herself, Marie stood there wondering what the Major thought he was up to. Then she started off slowly towards the bus queue. She looked back to see if a bus was coming and saw Joe on his scooter roaring round the corner. She stepped out into the road and waved wildly at him.

"Hallo," he said lightly. "Fancy seeing my little violet here. I've been scouring all the flower beds in London for you."

197

Marie clambered onto his pillion. "Take me back to school, Joe," she said grimly. "If you catch up with the Major, just ram him straight up his bumper for me."

Joe paused for a second, his foot ready on the kick-starter. "What's the Major to do with this?" he asked sharply. And Marie, too angry to give him a garbled version of the affair, as she normally would have done in order to avoid a humiliating confession, gave him a concise and accurate account of her dealings with the Major.

"And just why he wanted me in Kensington I don't know," she finished.

"He didn't care where you were, you goose," said Joe as he started the engine, "as long as you were out of the way. As far as he was concerned you were just a nuisance. You're not only nosey, but you've also got a curious and infuriating habit of popping up when you're not wanted." He moved away from the kerb and into the traffic, Marie clinging on as tightly as she could.

Meanwhile at school, Maggie had just finished her song and the whole audience was applauding enthusiastically, so enthusiastically in fact that Miss Fisher nodded at both Maggie and the pianist to sing the chorus again.

Fred sidled up to Miss Fisher and pushed a brown paper bag under her nose. "I've got the beads and things for the next scene," he hissed loudly. "Shall I give them to her?"

Miss Fisher swung round, her finger to her lips. She took the bag from him. "I'll do it," she whispered. "Go to your place. The soldiers will be on soon. Don't forget your lines."

Fred tagged on to the end of the file and marched on to the stage in a military manner. Unfortunately he was concentrating so hard on starting with his left foot that he didn't actually notice the boy in front moving off, so that Miss Fisher was forced to give him a shove to start him off.

Bobby sat bolt upright as he saw Fred appear and he lifted his puppet high above his head so that they could have a good look at each other. Fred turned and faced the audience. He pointed woodenly at the battlements where the ogre and the princess were going to appear. "See!" he bellowed, and then he stopped as a bar of light from outside illuminated the hall for a second or two as Harbottle entered it. Startled, Fred swung his arm round in a great arc and pointed directly at Harbottle. "He's here!" he exclaimed excitedly.

The audience looked blankly at each other. There was a subdued murmur of voices and the rasping of chairs as a number of people turned round. The cast was thrown out of its stride and they stared wildly at one another until Alan with great presence of mind moved smoothly to the centre of the stage and repeated Fred's line correctly. There were a number of nervous, self-conscious coughs and a few more whispers before the feeling of restlessness in the air died away and all attention was concentrated once more on the stage. All attention that is, but Bobby's. He began to slide slowly and silently from his seat to the floor, moving so gradually that his mother, now completely absorbed in the play again, didn't notice that he was gone.

Although the hall was quite dark except for the glow from the footlights and the stronger brilliance of the spots, Harbottle had left the door open just long enough for him to catch a glimpse of Bobby and mentally mark his position. Quietly and unhurriedly, he moved to the side of the hall and leaned back against the wall, his arms folded, utterly relaxed. He glanced at the stage. Maggie had been disturbed at the interruption, but she was now making a valiant attempt to pull herself together and the rest of the cast were backing her up as hard as they could.

Harbottle, bored by it all, looked back at Bobby's seat.

The chair was empty. Bobby had gone. Harbottle was mystified. Where could the kid have gone? He certainly couldn't be far away. There hadn't been time. His eyes flickered nervously across the audience and then suddenly he spotted him. This time Bobby was sitting much nearer the front, gazing innocently at the stage.

Harbottle heaved a great sigh. There was only one thing to do. Very carefully, moving slowly and as silently as he could, he edged his way down towards the front so that he was within range of Bobby once again. Suddenly the curtains fell and he slipped hastily into one of the few free seats near him.

The end of the scene was the beginning of the interval, and as the lights went up Harbottle picked up a programme and pretended to be absorbed in it. There was a great deal of clatter and movement around him and after a minute or two he felt it was safe enough for him to look around. The Major wasn't there, of course, he thought bitterly. Trust him to stay all snug and cosy in his great posh car while he, Harbottle, had to do all the dirty work as usual, fighting his way through women and children so that he could steal from a kid. And what thanks would he get when it was all over? None! All he'd get for his trouble would be a load of biting sarcasm. Simple job, that's what the Major called it, a simple job. He'd like to see the Major try it, that's all. It was about as simple as climbing Mount Everest. That Bobby was as slippery as an eel. He decided to keep his eye on him right through the interval.

Backstage Miss Fisher paused to comfort Maggie. "Don't worry, Maggie," she said. "It was going beautifully until the last few minutes. It's got nothing to do with you. I could tell the audience took to you from the first moment you stepped on the stage." She squeezed Maggie's shoulders affectionately. "Stick it in the back of your mind," she said. "Just remember how much they liked you."

"It didn't last long though, did it?" said Maggie miserably as Miss Fisher hurried off again.

"It was all right until Fred got his line wrong," Alan pointed out. "You knew it perfectly just before we started, Fred. What came over you?"

"It was suddenly seeing him standing there," Fred explained.

"Seeing who?" asked Leo, shaking a bit more powder in his hair.

"Harbottle. I just couldn't help it. I was staggered when I saw him come in."

"Oh, you are a twit," said Alan crossly, "a number one twit. What on earth does it matter who comes?"

Leo put down the powder and started patting his beard anxiously to make sure it was firmly anchored on his chin. "It's a bit funny though, when you come to think about it. I would have thought a bit of bovver in a back alley was more his cup of tea."

Miss Fisher returned. "Well, at least there is one bit of good news," she said, smiling. "The head of another school is here and he has asked if we will put the play on for them." Maggie's face brightened. "We'll be on stage again in a few minutes. Have you changed your belt and shoes, Maggie? Oh, good. Take off those pearls and we'll thread your mother's glass beads through your hair. Oh, they are lovely, aren't they? They are really beautiful." She wove the glittering red beads in and out of Maggie's hair while Maggie clasped the two heavy bracelets on her arm. Miss Fisher stood back and looked at her. "Now you really do look like a princess. Anyone would think you had got the crown jewels on."

The lights were turned out and the audience settled down as the volume of music was turned up. Maggie's mother,

having got Bobby back, now had him by her side once more
and was clutching one hand tightly so that he couldn't slip
away from her again. Bobby, his puppet gripped tightly in his
other hand, wriggled round from time to time to stare
anxiously at Harbottle. He tugged fruitlessly at his mother's
hand until she whispered crossly that she would smack him if
he didn't keep still. Harbottle, now in a seat almost
immediately behind them and only two rows away, sat there
as inconspicuously as possible and awaited his chance.

About ten minutes later he glanced at the faces around
him. They were completely absorbed in the play. Stealthily,
he leaned forward as far as he could. It would be a bit of a
stretch, he reckoned, but he could just about do it. Silently
he half lifted himself from his seat and fumbled across the
heads of the people in front of him. His roving fingers
touched Bobby's hair first and then, as Bobby screamed, he
felt the puppet. With a tug he grabbed hold of it and Bobby
screamed again. Suddenly the lights down one side of the hall
were switched on. As the audience turned round, Harbottle
pushed his way through the row to the centre aisle and
looked round quickly for the best way out. The door he had
come in by was guarded by two boys but there was another
in the corner by the far side of the stage. He ran for it as
Bobby, his face scarlet, and wailing loudly, jumped to his feet
and pointed his finger at him. There was a babble of voices
and the scraping of chairs as people tried to see what was
going on.

"It's Harbottle!" cried Fred, rushing onto the stage. "Stop
him!" The audience reacted slowly. Harbottle got to the
front long before anyone had made a move. He rushed past
the edge of the stage, the puppet clasped closely to him, just
as Leo got to his feet. Fred made a desperate grab at his
jacket but he was too late and too far away, and so Harbottle

reached the safety of the door. Behind him the uproar increased and he could just hear the threatening sounds of men's voices as he hurled himself through it.

Maggie, still in her white dress, the red beads glowing in her hair, rushed onto the stage as she heard Bobby's screams while the pianist, in a vain attempt to restore some sort of order, struck up a rousing march just as the gramophone was switched on. Chairs were dragged backwards and forwards and knocked over. Little children began crying and sobbing in sympathy with Bobby. The protesting voices of mothers became shriller and the angry rumble of men's voices grew louder.

The soldiers tumbled carelessly onto the stage, knocking into each other and into anything else in their path. There was a sudden loud creak and a rumble as slowly and majestically the battlements swayed backwards and forwards. Gradually they gathered momentum and then, with a hideous grinding screech, they crashed to the ground and lay there quivering. In the moment of silence that followed only Leo's voice could be heard echoing round the hall. "Catch him!"

He leapt down with Alan close behind him while Fred, his rifle clutched like a club, scrambled down after them. The rest of the cast poured off the stage, grabbing at anything that seemed a likely weapon. The Queen, long skirts in one hand and a stool in the other, pelted after the boys, while the King, sword in hand, completely oblivious of the fact that it was constructed of cardboard and silver paper, charged after her. The dragon capered after them. In one scaly paw was a fairy's wand, while the other grasped his tail in a vain attempt to stop it from dragging along the ground. Maggie scopped up Bobby and trotted along by his side.

Down the corridor ran Harbottle. He paused for a moment

at the end of it, wondering which was the best way out. Suddenly he realised he had to go through the narrow cloakroom and so he pounded on. His momentary hesitation lost him part of the lead, for as he went out the cast rushed in. He gained a little time as they became jammed in the cloakroom and jostled and shoved at each other in an effort to be the first out. Harbottle fled to the gates where he was hampered for a few seconds by a woman who was blocking the way with a pram. They each shuffled backwards and forwards in a sort of insane dance, trying to make room for each other, until Harbottle managed to squeeze through.

As he looked back he saw Alan careering out into the playground, closely followed by a whooping horde of children. With a horrified look on his face, Harbottle took to his heels again and swerved round the nearest corner.

Alan shot round after him, but slipped and fell into the gutter. Fred galloped past him breathing heavily as if he were a racehorse and Leo, snorting as pieces of his beard flew up his nose, hurtled after him. Alan got up and joined the Queen, who now had only one leg of the stool left, but was gripping it in a very determined manner. The dragon, who had pushed his mask up a bit in order to breathe more easily, found that he now had two mouths and almost no vision and so missed the corner completely and trotted gamely up the Portobello Road all on his own, staggering and tumbling into anyone unfortunate enough to get in his way.

Harbottle rounded yet another corner and then immediately darted into a narrow alley. He stood there, utterly still and holding his breath, largely obscured by an upturned barrow, and watched the strangely-dressed mob rush past. He waited for a second or two and then tugged his clothes straight and strode out to double back on his tracks. Breathing a little more easily, he confidently swung round the corner and came face to face with Maggie and Bobby.

"Mine!" shouted Bobby, stretching out his hand as Harbottle swerved past them and started to run again.

"Here!" screamed Maggie. "Help!" She stood still long enough for the stragglers from the procession to turn back as she waved violently at them. As they retraced their steps she turned and rushed after Harbottle again. She saw him dodging across the road and guessed where he was going. She saw the boys in the distance. "St Peter's Square!" she yelled and saw them rush down the nearest back alley in order to make a short cut. She chased after Harbottle across the waste ground to the square and there, its engine ticking over quietly, was the sleek, powerful, gleaming Jaguar. Alan and Fred galloped madly towards it with Leo close behind. Maggie, still some distance away, stood dejectedly as Harbottle scrambled into it. With a roar of its powerful engine, the car leapt into life and zoomed away round the corner.

"Beaten! He's beaten us," panted Alan.

"My puppet!" wailed Bobby.

Leo tugged his beard off and threw it on the ground in disgust. "We've lost."

Fred grinned. "He can't get out that way," he said. "They've got the road up. He's got to come round again."

Maggie looked round desperately. "We've got to stop them. What can we do?"

"Nothing," replied Alan grimly.

They stood silently at the exit to the square. They could hear the roar of the engine as the car raced back. It got closer and closer, and then the gleaming car shot past them once more. They all leapt backwards. Fred hurled his useless rifle at it and they all watched it hit the door, bounce off and fall into the road. Despondently they stared as the car hurtled round the last corner. They stood together, a silent defeated little crowd.

And then suddenly there was a hideous whining screech of brakes and a screaming of tyres, a prolonged metallic clatter, a jangle of machinery, a horrible grating and then finally, a thunderous crash. There was silence and then the gentle sound of tinkling glass.

Alan was the first to realise what had happened. "Come on!" he yelled triumphantly. "Come on! We've got them!"

They hurled themselves round the corner and there, almost in front of them, was the Jaguar, its beautiful body crumpled and crushed against a wall, a motor scooter crunched beneath its front wheels. The driver was slumped in his seat and Joe, leaning across him, had his head in the window and was happily playing with the dashboard. Harbottle was being removed from the passenger seat by a constable and Marie was hugging Bobby's puppet.

They all clustered round the car. "Your scooter, Joe!" cried Maggie. "It's ruined."

Joe took his head out of the car. "It doesn't matter," he said. "Gas lamps are on their way out."

"He pushed me off," said Marie. "He aimed the scooter straight at it. He only just escaped himself."

Harbottle cast a vicious look at the puppet. "That perishing thing," he said. "I always said it was a mistake to put the jewels in that perishing thing."

The Major stirred slightly and then, with great effort, he raised his head to look contemptuously at Harbottle. "You'll never learn to keep that great mouth of yours shut, will you?" he said wearily. "You'll never learn."

Harbottle twisted round and glared at him, an ugly expression on his face. "It's the same old story, isn't it? You play the gent while I do the dirty work. You wouldn't soil

206

your hands, would you? Let me tell you we'd have got away all right if you hadn't been such a lousy rotten driver. I'd got that perishing puppet, hadn't I?"

"That puppet," drawled the Major, "would have been as much use to us as a lantern would be to a blind man." His mouth twisted in a rueful smile.

"What the hell do you mean?" demanded Harbottle.

"Just look at our little princess," said the Major, as a policeman hauled him out of the car.

Everyone turned and stared at Maggie. She looked at them in alarm and played nervously with the tassels of her belt. "I don't know what he means," she said uneasily.

Joe carefully untwined the red beads from her hair and then unclasped the heavy bracelets. "Hey presto and abracadabra and all that," he said as he handed them over to a policeman. "The missing rubies are missing no longer."

Rubies! They all looked stunned. Fred recovered himself first. "You can't do that," he said truculantly. "I got them out of Maggie's house. They're her Mum's."

Joe smiled. "I rather think Bobby discovered them first and hid them," he said, "and then you picked them up by mistake, Fred. You did hide the beads, didn't you, Bobby?"

"Yes," said Bobby absently. He was engaged on a careful examination of the puppet. He wanted to make sure that it had come to no harm.

"But Bobby found the puppet in the Portobello," pointed out Leo. "He couldn't have stuffed the rubies in it."

"If you remember, he found it near their best friend's stall and their best friend was found to have the empty jewel case in his possession. He could hardly have the rubies on display, now could he? He had to conceal them somewhere until it was safe to flog them, and that meant that he had to hide them in something that no one could possibly want."

"I did," said Bobby.

There were a number of police around by now. One of them tugged Joe's hair in a friendly way. "Watcher, Goldilocks," he said. "Lucky you're not in Inspector Smith's division or you would have been the first hippie in history with a short back and sides."

Joe grinned back at him. "Hippie!" he said. "You're out of touch, pal. This is considered ordinary civilian gear in my division." He turned back to them. "Why don't you all nip off and change? We can all meet later and sort things out."

Fred looked up. "Then I was right," he said. "I was right all the time and you lot thought I was just being daft."

Marie glanced at him. "So you were, Fred," she said in an astonished tone. "You were right all along."

"Right about what?" asked Leo.

"I kept saying they were after the puppet," shouted Fred.

"Did you now?" said Joe, regarding him with interest. "I'll tell you what, Fred. You look absolutely splendid in that uniform. There's no need for you to change. Why not come to the copper shop with me and we'll see those two safely stashed away and then we'll have a cup of tea in the canteen together." He turned to the rest of the group who were standing in astounded silence. "We'll meet you in El Tropicana in about three quarters of an hour."

"But what about me?" cried Marie. "I'm ready."

"Then you can go and help Maggie. Be her dresser. Help her in your usual kind and thoughtful manner. Maybe you'll even store up a little credit for yourself in heaven," and he sauntered off with his arm round the shoulder of a delighted, scarlet-faced Fred.

"Why are you taking Fred?" asked Marie jealously.

"Because he's one of us," said Joe. "We 007s must stick together."